THE NAME ON
THE BRACELET

"COME DOWN HERE, MISS," THE MAN CALLED LOUDLY.
JUDY'S HEART MISSED A BEAT.

The Name on the Bracelet   *Frontispiece (Page 123)*

A JUDY BOLTON MYSTERY

THE NAME ON THE BRACELET

BY

MARGARET SUTTON

ILLUSTRATED BY

PELAGIE DOANE

GROSSET & DUNLAP
PUBLISHERS   NEW YORK

To Helen Dichl Olds,
Affectionately Known as "Pick"

The Famous JUDY BOLTON *Mystery Stories*

By MARGARET SUTTON

In Order of Publication

CONTENTS

CHAPTER I

A DISTURBANCE AT NIGHT

JUDY BOLTON awakened with a start. She felt sure she had heard a door opening and closing somewhere in the house. She glanced at her alarm clock. It was a few minutes after two, she could see by the illuminated face. But perhaps it was only her father, the doctor, who had received one of his frequent night calls.

Whatever it was, the sound had startled her into wakefulness and she felt she must investigate. But she wouldn't wake her father. She would simply go down to the office and see if he was there. If she found him, that would explain it. But if she didn't—well, anyway, she'd have a look.

In the hall she almost collided with her brother, Horace. He was wearing a black and white striped beach robe, but all she could see was the white stripes.

"You look like an escaped convict," she declared. "What are you doing up at this hour of the night?"

"I heard something," he said, raising a warning finger. "Didn't you?"

"A door closing. That was all. Who else is up?"

"You and me, I guess. That's all. But considering the house's reputation and not having a single good story to turn in to the paper, I thought the least I could do was to investigate."

"That's just what I was doing," Judy said. "Come on."

A catcall came weirdly from the lower hall as they descended the stairs.

"Blackberry," Judy whispered, "and I'm sure I put him out."

"Someone's let him in," said Horace logically as Judy picked up her pet and began stroking him. Little sparks of electricity from the cat's fur crackled in the darkness.

"For Pete's sake, stop it!" Horace exploded. "If you want light, turn on your flash."

"Good idea," Judy agreed as she directed the round beam of light toward the living room. The door was closed, but the door to her father's office on the opposite side was standing open—a thing which never happened. Usually it was locked for it was here that the doctor kept his files and important records as well as his various medicines and equipment. But apparently nothing had been touched.

The wind was blowing a gale outside the house. It whistled through the old trees and shook their branches. Inside, the window shade was flapping back and forth, making a sound that was almost like someone tapping against the glass.

Judy listened a moment and then pointed.

"Is the wind doing that too?" she asked.

Horace followed the direction of her finger.

"I don't see anything unusual," he said. "Naturally, the wind would make the window shade flap back and forth."

"*If* the window happened to be open," Judy told him. "But this window isn't open. It's closed and locked. Dad always locks his office windows."

"Well, it can't be—" Horace began.

But Judy, with a quick pull, had snapped the shade clear to the top of the window.

"Look!" she exclaimed. "Just as I thought. The window's broken!"

"Now how could that have happened?"

"It wasn't an accident; that's sure," Judy declared. "The break is right next to the lock so that someone could easily push up the window and sneak inside. Someone must have done it too. How else did Blackberry get in the house after I put him out?"

"Gosh!" said Horace. "Then we will have to wake Mother and Dad."

"That won't be necessary, Son," said the

kindly voice of Dr. Bolton who already stood in the open doorway. "I heard you two prowling around and suspected something was happening. Then I glanced out of the window and saw a man just vaulting over the hedge. He wasn't carrying anything so whatever he took must have been small enough to go in his pocket. Your mother is just calling the police from the upstairs phone."

"You had the jump on us, didn't you, Dad?" said Horace with a grin.

Judy's gray eyes shone. "It's another mystery," she announced. "Peter and I are going to have a lot of fun solving it."

"What about me?" Horace asked. "Don't I come in on this mystery business too? Just because Peter's a lawyer, he doesn't have a monopoly on mysteries. My paper likes a good mystery write-up too."

"We'll solve it together then. I'll tell Peter about it tomorrow morning when I go to the office. In the meantime, we might look for clues. You don't see any initialed handkerchiefs or signet rings laying around, do you?"

"Burglars don't leave such things except in stories."

"Oh, is that so, smarty? Well, I bet *I* can find something. This *is* going to be fun——"

"It may be fun for you young people," the doctor told them seriously. "But it means hard work and worry for me. I see where I shall have to spend the rest of the night going over my files to make sure no records have been touched. I don't see why they would be, I admit. But I must make sure. And still more important, I shall have to check every bottle of medicine. I certainly don't want to be responsible for any dangerous drugs in the hands of criminals."

"Oh, Dad! I'm sorry," Judy said. "I didn't think of that. Could I help you?"

"I'm afraid not," he answered. "That's something I shall have to do myself. Now you two either skedaddle back to bed or continue your investigation somewhere else."

"In the kitchen," Horace whispered. "That must have been the door you heard closing. All the other doors in this half of the house were left open."

The house was built with a hall through the center and the kitchen at the back. Thus one of the kitchen doors opened into the doctor's quarters while the other led into the dining room. Judy and Horace disappeared through one of these doors and Blackberry followed them.

Judy started toward the refrigerator to see if there was any milk left, but stopped perfectly still at the sound of a wailing police siren outside. In another moment she heard her father talking with Inspector Bird. She turned to Horace.

"Do you hear that voice?"

"We'll have a look around," the inspector was saying to their father. "Where's that son of yours who works on the *Herald?* And where's your daughter, the famous girl detective?"

"Sarcastic, isn't he?" commented Horace.

"Dumb is the word," said Judy.

She had never liked Inspector Bird and was quite sure he had no use for her. The chief of police, however, was quite fond of her. She wished he could have sent some other officer.

"You'll find the young folks in the kitchen," the doctor was saying. "They're investigating, I believe. But, so far as I can discover, nothing of importance has been touched."

"Sure it was a burglar and not just the cat that jumped through the window?"

The doctor laughed.

"I hardly see how a cat could have leaped through a pane of glass without cutting himself, do you, Inspector?"

Judy made a discovery just as Inspector Bird opened the kitchen door. She turned from the refrigerator where she was kneeling and exclaimed, "He had something to eat!"

She was speaking to Horace, but it was the inspector who answered her.

"Who had something to eat? The cat?"

"Why, yes—No, I mean," she stammered, a little startled at his sudden entrance. "Of course, the cat did have something. I just poured out a saucer of milk for him. But I mean the man—the one who came in through the window."

"How do you know it wasn't a female?"

"I don't know who it was," Judy admitted. "But I do know that he—well, *it* had something to eat."

"And how do you figure that?"

Judy exhibited an empty plate.

"There was a piece of pie on here," she said. "Our burglar must have eaten it. And I'm sure we had more than three pieces of ham left over from dinner."

"Don't touch anything," the inspector warned her, waving her out of the kitchen. "This may be more serious than it looks. We don't want to spoil any fingerprints."

"An embezzlement," joked Horace, the humorous story he would write for his paper already forming in his mind. "Some hungry guy broke into the house to embezzle a few slices of ham and a piece of pie."

"If that's all he took—and you can lay to it, it ain't— he still committed the crime of breaking and entering," snapped the inspector.

"*And* petty larceny?"

Judy turned to her brother.

"The whole thing is petty, if you ask me," she said with a yawn. "I won't be needed now that the inspector is solving everything. I think I'll go back to bed and get my beauty sleep."

"A fine idea," approved the inspector. "A pretty girl like you ought to be thinking of her looks. Now me," he continued, carefully dusting aluminum powder on the edge of the pie plate, "I got more important things to think about."

Judy almost giggled.

"You might spray the glass around that broken place in the window," she suggested over her shoulder. "It's just possible some member of the family ate the ham and the pie."

Her accusing glance, this time, was for Horace. She knew he often raided the ice box for a late snack before going to bed.

"That sister of yours!" groaned Bird, looking at Horace who was now wholly in sympathy with him.

Judy stopped only a moment to say good night to her father. He was busy, she could see, and she did not want to disturb him. In the morning, perhaps, he would have something to tell her. She did wish he would let her help him check his records and his medicines. She couldn't quite believe the burglar had stolen nothing except a few slices of ham and a piece of pie.

CHAPTER II

IN THE morning Judy dressed herself so that she looked quite grown-up and sophisticated. She felt that she owed it to herself after her little girl adventure of the night before.

"I'm really not a little girl any more," she told herself. "I'm grown up and so are all my friends. Of course, Selma Brady's still in high school. But Scottie's in college and Lorraine's engaged. And Irene—goodness! Irene has been married for nearly two years!"

It made Judy feel fairly ancient to think of Irene Lang—Irene Meredith now. They had been such chums but it had been nearly six months since Judy had even heard from her friend in New York. She hadn't been singing over the radio lately either and Judy wondered why. Irene had a beautiful voice and used to sing on a regular evening program. It had made Judy feel closer to the Cinderella girl, as she called her, to listen. But lately another voice had taken the place of "the golden voice of Irene Meredith" as the radio announcer described it.

9

"And she never answered my last letter," Judy remembered. "Now that's the sort of thing grown people wonder about. They aren't forever poking their noses into burglaries and haunted houses."

But when she thought of haunted houses a delicious shiver ran up and down Judy's spine. Houses weren't really haunted, of course, but when mysterious things happened in them it was fun to think they were. Several mysterious things had happened in Tower House, the queer old homestead Irene had inherited from her grandmother. She and her husband, Dale Meredith, the detective story writer, now lived there.

"I suppose they're like all married people by now," Judy thought. "Grown-up and settled." And, at that thought, being grown-up became a little less attractive to her. Yes, she thought, rather wistfully now, her little girl adventures were all behind her. Her friends were all grown up and she was—it sounded terribly drab and uninteresting in her present mood—yes, she was a secretary. She frowned at herself in the mirror, trying to look as stern as she felt a proper secretary should.

No, that wouldn't do. For, after all, she was Peter's secretary. And he still liked to poke his nose into mysteries and investigate burglaries and explore supposedly haunted houses.

It wasn't like being secretary to just anybody. Peter's secretary wouldn't frown. She'd be gay and cheerful.

"Like this," Judy decided, fastening a pale green jitterbug bow at the top of her head to hold together her mass of auburn curls.

There! She didn't look so grown-up after all.

She made a face at herself in the mirror and then skipped on down to breakfast. Horace looked up at her with a wide grin.

"I see you did get your beauty sleep."

"Thank you," she said, "if that's a compliment. But I couldn't do anything else after Inspector Bird practically told me to go to bed—like a child," she added. "But I'm grown up this morning. I really think I'm too old to get excited over a mystery."

Horace nearly choked over his egg. But Judy only looked at him as though she were the older of the two and not the younger.

For several moments after that they ate in silence, Judy's mother at one end of the table, her father at the other and the two young people at one side. The table was pushed against the wall except when they had company for, if there was one thing the doctor insisted upon, it was space in which to move about. But presently the silence was interrupted by Horace's outrageous parrot shrieking, "What's the racket?" It was an expression he frequently used but, at the moment, it seemed peculiarly appropriate.

Horace jumped out of his chair and shook his fist at the parrot in mock rage, but as he did so, he pulled the table a little away from the wall.

"Hey!" objected the doctor. "You're spilling my coffee."

"And you need it after last night, don't you, Dad?" Judy said sympathetically.

Judy's mother gave a little start.

"What's that? Did you drop something, Horace?"

"No, I didn't drop anything." Horace's face was a blank.

"I was sure I heard something," Mrs. Bolton said. "It sounded like some kind of a paper or book slipping down behind the table."

"Mo-other!" Judy exclaimed and made one dive underneath the table. The rest of the family held onto their plates and saucers and Horace could not resist the comment:

"And Judy was too old to get excited over a mystery!"

Meanwhile Judy had retrieved the article her mother had heard falling. She looked at it—and then stared. It was a bankbook and the name on the cover was that of a New York savings bank. The account belonged to Ludwig Bull. Now who was he? And how would his bankbook get wedged in between the kitchen table and the wall?

"What is it?" Horace asked, unable to conceal his curiosity a moment longer.

"A bankbook," Judy answered. "Dad, do you know anyone named Ludwig Bull?"

The doctor thought a minute.

"No, Judy. It's an unusual name and I'm sure I would recognize it if I knew the person——"

"Then you don't know him!" exclaimed Judy. "And if none of the rest of us know him, then there's just one way this bankbook could have been left here. It was left here by our hungry thief."

"Aw, Judy. They just don't go together——" Horace began.

"Let me see the bankbook," Dr. Bolton interrupted.

He opened it and discovered a list of several deposits and withdrawals, leaving a balance of well over two thousand dollars.

"With all that money, he couldn't have been very hungry," Horace said, looking over his shoulder.

"But he must have dropped it," Judy insisted. "He must have sat right at this table to eat his piece of pie and then, when he got up, a corner of the table or something must

have knocked the bankbook out of his pocket.
And you were the one," she added with a look
at Horace, "who said burglars never left initialed handkerchiefs and signet rings except
in stories."

"Well, this is a bankbook——"

"Yes, and it's just as good as a calling card.
Dad, I know it's unreasonable of me, but I'd
give anything if I could return this bankbook
to Ludwig Bull myself."

"That's impossible, Judy. You can see the
account is with a New York bank. He probably lives in New York," her father told her.

"Then what's his bankbook doing here,
Dad?"

"I'd like to know the answer to that question
myself," declared Dr. Bolton. "The whole
thing is something of a puzzle. I went over
everything very carefully last night and all
my belongings seem to be exactly as I left them.
I made absolutely certain that no drugs had
been handled. In fact, my medicine cabinet
was locked and the key just where I had placed
it. The patients' cards and case records all
checked with each other and none of my instru-
ments had been disturbed. And yet this bankbook confirms Inspector Bird's opinion that a
professional burglar broke through that window. A desperately hungry person would

hardly have two thousand dollars on deposit in a bank."

"The hungry thief made a good newspaper story anyway," said Horace. "Just wait until you see it in the papers. I telephoned it in at four o'clock."

"So that accounts for your haggard expression," joked Judy. "You were up all night writing an essay."

"Call it that if you like," Horace returned. "It was pretty long. But even if they cut it down to half its size, it will still be hot stuff. Golly! Is that a telegraph messenger boy turning in at our gate?"

Mrs. Bolton's hand went to her heart. She had never gotten over the feeling that a telegram was sure to carry bad news. But Judy, eager and expectant, ran to the door.

"Telegram for Miss Judy Bolton. Are you Miss Bolton? Sign here," the boy said all in one breath as he thrust the yellow envelope into her hand.

Judy tore it open and read:

JUDY IRENE MEREDITH BORN THIS MORNING LETTER FOLLOWS

DALE

It was a minute before Judy grasped the

meaning of the message. Judy Irene Meredith? Why, it was both their names!

"Well, what is it?" Judy's mother asked anxiously.

"Oh, Mother! The grandest news!" Judy cried out joyously. "Irene has a baby and she's named it after me!"

"Little Irene," Mrs. Bolton murmured as though it were sad instead of happy news.

"Oh, but isn't it wonderful?" Judy ran on excitedly. "I've been wondering why Irene had stopped singing on the radio and why she didn't write or anything. But it was because of this baby. And she's named it Judy—Judy Irene Meredith."

"A namesake! Well, that is something," said Dr. Bolton, looking as proud as though it had been his own grandchild.

"I'll put it in the paper," Horace declared. "Everyone in Farringdon will be glad to hear that there is another Judy. I wonder if she will be anything like you."

"I don't see how she could be," laughed Judy. "Irene and I are as different as black and white. But, of course, there's Dale. I always thought we were something alike. He writes mysteries and I solve them and—Oh, Dad! Why couldn't I solve this one? I could go to New York and return the bankbook myself and visit little Judy Irene."

"I suppose you do want to visit her, don't you, Judy girl?" Dr. Bolton asked.

"Of course. I never wanted anything so much in my life. Mother, how soon would it be all right for me to go?"

"Wait and see what Dale says in his letter," Judy's mother advised. "Then, if Peter can spare you from the office——"

"He can! I know he can," Judy interrupted. "Only the other day he was asking me if I didn't want my vacation. I didn't have one last summer, you remember, because of that Vincent case."

"And you told him?"

"Foolish me!" Judy chided herself. "I told him I didn't. I told him that no vacation could possibly be as much fun as helping him solve his cases. But this telegram has made me change my mind and I'm sure he'll let me go. He must realize how much I want to see my own namesake. Oh, goody! There he is now."

And, grabbing her hat and coat, Judy rushed down the walk to tell Peter about little Judy Irene.

CHAPTER III

JUDY had known Peter Dobbs since they were both children in Roulsville. The town had been flooded and both families had moved to Farringdon, a much larger town. But, with the real estate boom in Roulsville, Peter had returned to establish his law office there. It was not a pretentious office. The one-story brick building with the name PETER DOBBS, ATTORNEY AT LAW, on the door looked something like a toy office such as a child might construct out of building blocks. But it suited Peter all right. He was an honest young man with nothing to hide and had no need of a private reception room. His clients, he hoped, were honest too. At any rate he was quite willing that Judy should hear anything they had to tell him. If he had any doubts about a case, he always asked her advice. Usually they discussed such things as they were driving to work together. But today Judy was bubbling over with news of her own. First she had to tell Peter all about her new namesake. Then she related the story of the hungry thief who had broken into her father's office and then entered the kitchen and helped himself to ham and pie.

"And that isn't all," Judy added. "This morning when we were eating breakfast Mother heard something slipping down behind the table and what do you suppose it was? A bankbook that the hungry thief had left behind him as a clue! And Dad says he doesn't care if I return it to him. Anyway, he didn't say he did care. And so I'm going to New York and visit my namesake and solve a mystery besides. Isn't it going to be the grandest vacation?"

But, somehow, Peter wasn't as delighted with the news she gave him as Judy thought he would be.

"I'll miss you, Judy," he said. "But, of course, you deserve a vacation and things are a little quiet at the office. How soon do you expect to leave?"

"I suppose I'll have to wait a little while, won't I?" she asked. She hadn't thought of that. "But I'll start clearing up things this morning," she added brightly. "I'll put your files in order and we'll answer all the old correspondence——"

She had forgotten that they were going to close up the office and go for a ride in the afternoon. And all morning, as she hurried about the work in the office, she never noticed how longingly Peter's eyes followed her. She was thinking only of her coming vacation as she banged away at the typewriter or bent her curly head over the files.

A talkative client came in about noon and kept them both until long after lunchtime. But when the door closed behind him, Peter turned and said, "I call this a good day's work, if it did take only a morning. Now let's knock off for lunch and take the afternoon off. I had something to tell you and it's waited long enough."

"That's right. You did," Judy agreed, pulling the cover over her typewriter.

"Lunch?" Peter suggested when they were in the car.

"Let's have hamburgers at a road stand."

"And ice cream," he added. "We must, at least, have ice cream. I had planned to take you to the Yellow Bowl, only it isn't very private."

Now Judy did look at him. The Yellow Bowl was Farringdon's most exclusive eating place. But it would be three o'clock before they could possibly be there—and Judy was hungry.

"We don't have to make an occasion of it, do we?" she asked. "We nearly always have lunch together. It's nothing new. And I'm not fussy. Here's Joe's place. He has good hamburgers. Let's stop."

Peter looked a little disappointed as he climbed out of the car. Judy couldn't imagine

why. A moment later, however, he returned
with two sizzling hot hamburgers clapped between rolls and a paper bag which held two
Dixie cups. His face was wreathed in smiles.

"I have an idea. We'll eat on the picnic
tables out there."

He indicated two tables which had been
placed out under the trees so that summer
tourists might eat their lunches there. It was
now late Autumn and the tables were deserted.
But Judy and Peter were warmly dressed and
the sun was shining through the almost naked
trees. Peter spread the car blanket over one of
the benches and motioned for Judy to sit down.

"Like it?" he asked when he had returned
again with steaming cups of coffee.

"Love it!" she exclaimed. "I'd live in the
woods if it were possible. I wonder if the
leaves turn so many glorious colors anywhere
else in the world."

"They're like your hair," he commented, intending a compliment.

"Red, you mean?"

"I guess I'm not very romantic, am I?" he
asked, suddenly confused.

Judy surveyed him critically—his blunt
nose, his hair which would never stay in place,
his wide mouth. She shook her head.

"Hardly. But you have a nice face. I like
it."

"So well that you'd want to look at it for the

rest of your life? Over the breakfast table, I
mean, and—and—Oh, heck! You know what
I'm trying to tell you, Judy. I've told you before, but you never would take me seriously.
And now, if you're going away on a vacation,
maybe it wouldn't be right to ask you to promise. I never did like people doing things because they thought they had to.''

"Well,'' Judy asked, pleased as well as a
little amused by Peter's fumbling proposal,
"what is it that you want me to do?''

"I—'' He paused and cleared his throat,
then took a small, square box from his vest
pocket. "I just wanted you to wear this. It
was Grandmother's,'' he went on, opening the
box and revealing an exquisite old ring.
"Maybe you've seen her wearing it. She had
it on when the Roulsville dam broke and that's
how it happened to be saved. Well, it's a diamond and you like diamonds and you said you
liked old jewelry and—and if you like me——''

Judy stopped him with a kiss—a rather
hasty one, to be sure, for she suspected Joe was
watching them from his roadside stand.

"You dear silly!'' she half-scolded. "Of
course I like you. I've liked you ever since we
were kids. But that isn't all you want. You
want me to love you—and I think I do.''

"Then will you—will you wear the ring?''

"I shall be very proud to wear it,'' she answered softly. "It's so much more precious to

me because your grandmother wore it too.
But you know, Peter, I like working for you.
I like the office and all the cases that come up
and collecting evidence and all that. You
wouldn't want me to give up my work and—
and just keep house?"

"I hadn't figured it all out," Peter confessed. "I still have Grandma and Grandpa
to think of—and they're pretty old."

"Then isn't it like the Scotch song that goes:

'I canna leave the auld folk now;
We'd better bide a wee?'"

"But they wouldn't want that," Peter objected. "My grandparents would never stand
in the way of our happiness. They're fond of
you, Judy. Grandma herself said that she
wanted to live long enough to see us married
so that she could rest easier in her grave. It
was an odd way to put it, but you see what she
meant. That was why she gave me her engagement ring. She wanted to see you wearing it
while she was still alive."

"She's a dear!" Judy murmured. "They
both are. But Peter, it's this way. I'm still in
my 'teens and Dad says it's too young and
Mother agrees with him and, somehow, I feel
I'm not ready for marriage. I know something about law and a lot about mysteries but
precious little about housekeeping and babies.

What I mean is, maybe Irene could teach me a few things. Maybe I would be sure after I spent a couple of weeks with her. You see, Peter, when we are married, I want to make you happy."

"Then take your vacation and learn as much as you can. Dale and Irene are the happiest married couple I know."

"But they're not like us, Peter. Irene's delicate and Dale thinks he has to take care of her. I'd hate being taken care of."

"Don't worry, you won't be."

But Judy was too excited to retort to Peter's remark in her usual quick manner. She kept turning the ring he had given her around and around on her finger, imagining it was a wishing ring and would make her fondest dreams come true. Perhaps it was. Perhaps every girl felt that way about her engagement ring. But then Judy remembered another ring—the one Arthur Farringdon-Pett had given her. She hadn't felt that *his* ring was a wishing ring. She had given it back to him in the end and now Lorraine Lee was wearing it. But that was a secret. Lorraine must never know that her engagement ring had ever been on Judy's finger. Fortunately, she had kept everything to herself because she hadn't been quite sure.

"Peter," she asked, searching his face for an answer, "how can two people be sure they're the ones for each other? How do you and I know? What makes Arthur and Lorraine so sure? And how could Dale and Irene tell that, out of all the millions living in New York, they were meant for each other?"

Peter was stumped for an answer.

"You wouldn't be you, Judy, if you didn't make a mystery of it," he said.

"Well, it is a mystery," she returned. "Some married people are happy and some aren't and all of them thought they were going to be. They wouldn't have married each other if they hadn't thought they were going to be happy."

Peter drew a long sigh.

"I guess it's just a chance we take. But, to use an old expression of yours, I'm willing to bet something precious that you and I will make a go of it. We've done all right in the office together."

"That's different——"

"I *hope* so," he laughed, pulling her up from the bench before she could scrape the last bit of melted ice cream out of her cup. "Now shall we tell the folks?"

"Oh, lets!" cried Judy, two stars appearing in her gray eyes. Suddenly she wanted to dance and shout and tell the whole world. She was so glad it was Peter—dear Peter—and no one else. Maybe *that* was how you knew.

CHAPTER IV

THE FAREWELL PARTY

"Mother! Dad!" cried Judy, bursting through the front door. "What do you suppose has happened *now?* It wasn't enough for me to have another mystery to solve and a little namesake all my own. Now I'm going to have a *husband!*"

"A husband? What on earth?" gasped Mrs. Bolton.

"Why, Peter. Who else could it be? Who else did I ever really care about? Don't look so dumbfounded, Mother. You must have guessed he loved me and now he's given me a beautiful old ring that used to belong to his grandmother. It was her engagement ring too and she wants me to have it. So, you see, Peter and I are really engaged! And he's letting me have the vacation I wanted. Isn't it wonderful?"

"I hope you realize that being engaged is something more than just another adventure," said Dr. Bolton sternly.

"Why, Dad! Of course I do."

"You're such a child," Mrs. Bolton protested. "It seems hardly yesterday that you and Peter were playing hide-and-go-seek."

Her eyes were misty as she finished. "And now I'm going to lose my little daughter."

"Lose me!" Judy's eyes were wide and puzzled. "Why, what do you mean, Mother? I'm not going to *die*."

"Of course we won't lose her," Dr. Bolton said brusquely. "We're only adding a son to the family. Now, tell us, Judy, where do you young folks plan to live?"

Judy gave a start.

"Oh, goodness! We don't know. We're not married yet, Dad. We're just engaged."

"I never did approve of long engagements," said Mrs. Bolton, her voice still tearful. "You know, Judy, your father and I were married two weeks after he asked me. We were sure of what we wanted to do. But you and Peter— You're such children."

Judy's exhuberance had left her now. She had thought they would be as thrilled as she.

"Besides," her mother went on, "it seems a strange thing to me for a girl to become engaged and then take a vacation by herself. It seems to me that you and Peter would want to be together more than ever now."

"But I want to return the bankbook and— and see Irene's baby," Judy protested, almost in tears herself.

"That reminds me," said Dr. Bolton. "There's a letter from the baby's father there on the hall table."

"Oh, Dad! Why didn't you tell me before?"

But then Judy realized that she had hardly given him the chance to tell her anything. She tore open her letter eagerly and read:

Dear Judy:

I am sending this via air mail so that you will get it immediately and have time to plan accordingly. Irene has a request to make. She has taken it into her head that you are the only person in the world who can solve our nursemaid problem and has suggested that you come to Tower House for a visit.

Don't come if Peter finds he can not spare you from the office, but if he can, please, for Irene's sake, consider it at least. Irene has perfect confidence in you and I am sure you will be comfortable and happy with us until the nursemaid problem is settled. I can solve things on paper, but a problem like this takes a woman every time.

Wire us when to expect you and I will meet you. Doubtless you are eager to see your little namesake. So far, I have only peered at her through a glass window. I'm hoping for a better break when she is home the first of November. I am also hoping that we will have found a nursemaid soon after that.

With kindest regards,
Dale Meredith

As she studied the letter Judy understood it more and more clearly although, at first, it had seemed odd that Irene who had never done anything but work should require a nursemaid at all. Or why, if she did need one, it should be such a problem. But the Irene who sang on the radio, who entertained in a large, well-appointed house, was quite a different girl from the shabby little millworker Judy had first known.

"I guess I start practicing to be a housewife sooner than I expected," Judy said, handing her mother the letter. "One day I'm engaged and the next I'm hiring nursemaids. I suppose this means that they want me to be there by the first of November."

"I should think so," Mrs. Bolton agreed. "But are your clothes in shape, Judy? This is all happening so unexpectedly, I hardly know what to say."

"But of course she'll go," the doctor put in. "Peter has given her this vacation so that she may make the visit and I must admit, I'm curious to see what she can find out about that bankbook."

"I promise you, Dad, I'll find out something," Judy said, "if it's no more than telling you what this Bull person looks like."

Judy's mother reminded her of her clothes again the following morning and so she gath-

ered together everything that needed to be
cleaned—hat, gloves, suit and three dresses—
and started off with them bundled under her
arm. Because she looked more like a washer-
woman's helper than her father's daughter,
she managed to pass all the girls from Farringdon's smart set on her way to town. They had
all seen the notice of Judy Irene's birth in the
Herald and wanted to congratulate Judy for
her new namesake.

"I'm going to see her," Judy announced.
"That's why I'm having everything cleaned.
I'm leaving in time to be there November first."

Judy's friends planned a farewell party at
the Farringdon-Pett mansion on the night she
intended to leave. Judy expected to have
everything packed by then and had no idea
what she would wear until she was told it would
be a masquerade.

"Being so near the end of October," Lois
explained, "we thought we could combine farewell party, birthday party and Halloween.
Come as a witch and bring Blackberry, won't
you?"

Judy consented, planning to announce her
engagement at the party. But being an engaged girl was still more thrilling to her than
the idea of being married. The word "settled"
seemed to her to describe all married women
and, if there was one thing she wouldn't be, it
was "settled."

She told Peter nothing of these disturbing thoughts, however, and when Mrs. Dobbs kissed her and called her "my little granddaughter" she almost forgot them herself. Mr. Dobbs' memory was failing and he kept forgetting she wasn't still in school. Honey, Peter's sister, was the most enthusiastic of all.

"If only I could have had the party for you, Judy," she said. "But this apartment is so small and Grandma and Grandpa mind the noise. We can't have parties here, you see." And then, all at once as though it had nothing to do with what she had just been saying, Honey asked, "But Judy, where are you and Peter going to live?"

Was everyone going to ask her that? Judy began to wonder if she hadn't been a little hasty in accepting Peter's ring when their plans were so vague. But she did love him. She was sure of that, and the rest would work out for itself.

Things were brighter the night of the party when her parents announced her engagement and made everyone feel that they were just as proud and happy about it as she was. No one asked her where she and Peter meant to live. All her friends seemed to take it for granted that they would remain engaged and have linen showers and lingerie showers and every other kind of shower. That was the way it was with Arthur and Lorraine. But Peter was just

Peter to Judy. She couldn't say "my fiancé" with all the little airs Lorraine had. It didn't fit Peter. She liked him plain and a little awkward, just the way he was. She would have missed it if he hadn't spilled some of his coffee in his saucer and tripped once on the dance floor. She and Honey giggled over it and squeezed each other's hands and told everybody how wonderful it was that they were going to be sisters.

"I feel so close to all my friends now," Judy confided to a group of them around a game board. "Honey and I are going to be sisters and Irene has a baby named for me and you are all giving me a party——"

"It isn't a party without fortunes," Lois put in. "Remember how we had fortunes at your Halloween party, Judy, when you showed up the ghosts in the attic? Well, we're going to have fortunes too." She held up her hand. "Form in line, everybody!" she directed. "We're going to parade to the garden and pull a root——"

"Pull a *what?*" asked Horace, stepping closer.

"A root. You know, a carrot or a turnip or something like that. The kitchen garden is this way."

"But why?" everybody wanted to know as the queer procession of masked figures moved toward the garden.

"It's an old verse," Lorraine sang out.

> " 'On Allhallow's eve
>   When the hour is late,
>   Pull a root from the garden
>   And read your fate.' "

A few of those who had come to the garden protested that it wasn't Allhallow's eve and so it wouldn't work. But they were assured that it was all in fun anyway. They were to pull their roots and then carry them back to the lighted living room. Each person was to try and read his own fortune.

Horace held up a beet.

"Is my face red!" he exclaimed and then refused to say another word.

Arthur Farringdon-Pett and his sister, Lois, had each pulled a turnip. Arthur said that meant they would both spend the rest of their lives in Farringdon and vegetate.

"Ugh!" shuddered Judy. "That word is even worse than 'settled.' "

It was now her turn to display a vegetable. It was a carrot which started from one top and then branched into two roots.

"Twins!" everybody shouted before she had a chance to say a word.

"That's Judy and Peter being engaged," Arthur spoke up. "See, Lorraine has one nearly like it and that stands for our engagement, doesn't it. Lorraine?"

"If you say so," she laughed, tossing her golden head.

Peter glanced at Judy who stood frowning at her carrot as though it meant something different from any of their suggestions.

"Suppose we all keep quiet and let Judy tell us what fate she reads from the root she pulled," he said.

"Well," Judy began when the howl of agreement had subsided, "you all know I don't believe in fortunes or fate or any such nonsense. To me it means simply that two carrot seeds were planted too close together. They didn't have room to grow and so they got mixed up."

"So we're mixed up, are we?" joked Peter as they went in for refreshments.

"I didn't say we were. But something is going to be and if that fortune comes true," she added, laughing, "then I will hang out my shingle and pose as Judy, the Mystic. Peter, wouldn't you just love being married to a fortuneteller?"

"Would that be any worse than being married to someone who's forever running about solving mysteries?" asked Lorraine who was walking with Arthur just behind them.

"Get her to tell you about her latest one," he urged.

And so, while they all crowded around her at the table, Judy related once more the story of her experience with the hungry thief and how, later, she had found what she thought must be his bankbook.

"I'm going to New York," she finished, "and he must live there. I'll call on him and I'm sure having found his bankbook will be a perfectly good excuse for calling. Then, perhaps, I can find out why he thought it necessary to break into our house at night. That is, if I'm clever."

"You will be," Honey prophesied. "Write and tell me what happens, won't you?"

Judy promised to do so and left all her friends still talking about the mysterious Ludwig Bull. She was too late for the bus she had planned to take, but there was another one at two o'clock. Peter drove her to the station and they sent Dale a telegram from there.

"Don't stay too long," Peter warned her as the bus was ready to start. "I'll be counting the days."

Judy waggled her finger with its precious ring.

"I'll have this to remind me of home—and you," she added. "Bye, Peter. By-ee!"

And she kept on throwing kisses from the bus window until Peter was out of sight.

CHAPTER V

SHOPPING FOR TWO

JUDY had boarded the bus at ten o'clock and by eleven she was fast asleep on the pillow that had been "twenty-five cents all the way to New York."

The bus rattled and rumbled up hilly roads and down again but Judy slept on. She never found it difficult to sleep on trains and buses—only at home when she was puzzling over some mystery. Now there was nothing to puzzle over until she had met Ludwig Bull, whoever he was, and started interviewing nursemaids for Judy Irene. Then, she knew, there would be plenty. She might as well rest while she had the chance.

Her dreams, what she remembered of them, were of Peter. They were working on a case together and Blackberry was in the office stamping all the legal documents with his paw. She would miss Blackberry. Funny, she thought drowsily as the bus entered the Holland tunnel, how you left one thing you liked to see another and always missed something. Wherever you

were, you missed something because you could
be in only one place at a time. But that was a
sleepy thought. Judy sat up in her seat now,
wide awake. Hurriedly she began collecting
her things. Why, she must have slept through
the whole trip! They were almost at the Penn
terminal and Dale was supposed to meet her
there.

"I look a sight," she told her reflection in the
little mirror she pulled from her purse.

But she jerked her hat on over her touseled
hair, dabbed a little powder on her nose and
noticed an improvement. Through the window
she could see Dale—tall, dark and handsome as
Irene always laughingly described him. He
was pacing up and down as though he had something on his mind.

"Well, Judy! You came at last," he greeted
her heartily the moment she stepped from the
bus.

A porter took the bags and Dale asked to
have them checked.

"Aren't we going to take them home?" Judy
asked.

Dale looked concerned and then began asking
things which seemed to have nothing to do with
her question.

"Did you rest well on the bus? How did you
leave your mother and father? You weren't

working too hard at the office, were you, in order to have things finished up before the trip?"

"Why, no," Judy answered at last. "What makes you ask? I'm rested. Do I look so terrible?"

He laughed at that. "You look fine. I was just thinking, if you really are rested, we might do a little shopping while we're so near the stores. You see, I don't know much about baby clothes and Irene is leaving the hospital this afternoon. She asked me to buy a bunting."

"I'd love to shop with you!" Judy exclaimed. "In fact, I intended to do a little running around myself—looking someone up and buying a few things for myself, you know. But that can wait. I suppose Irene wants a pink bunting. Pink is for girls. I know the kind— all wooly and warm with a little peak at the top."

"Yes, that's it," Dale agreed. "In fact, she wants two."

"Two buntings! Don't tell me it's twins!"

Judy was thinking of her carrot with the double root. But, of course, Dale would have let her know.

"Oh, no. Nothing like that," he assured her as they walked up Thirty-fourth Street toward the department stores. "But Irene has a friend. You may think it queer to make friends like that in the hospital. But she is in what they call a semi-private room. She wanted it that way so she wouldn't be so lonely. Well, as I was saying, these two have struck up quite a friendship. This other girl has a baby too—born the same day as little Judy Irene. But the father hasn't seen it. In fact, he hasn't shown much interest in it. The girl expected him to bring its clothes and he hasn't shown up. She is leaving the hospital and, naturally, the baby must be dressed."

"Naturally," Judy agreed, "and so you offered to help. I think it was real sweet of you, Dale, and I'll be glad to shop for the extra things."

"It won't be any trouble, ordering two of everything instead of one."

"But do you want the two babies dressed exactly alike?" questioned Judy.

"Why not?" said Dale, dismissing the matter with a gesture of his hand. "It's easier."

The buntings were just as Judy had imagined them—soft pink with a little pointed hood. They were pink inside and white outside.

"Like rabbits' ears," commented Judy.

"We'll take two," Dale told the salesclerk.

"Twins?" she beamed. "How delightful!"

Dale gave her a dark look and went on to the next counter where they bought shirts, diapers and two little dresses. The dresses were perfectly plain except for a row of pink feather-stitching around the neck. Then Judy thought of booties and bought two pair of white knitted ones with pink ribbon bows.

"What else does a baby wear?" Dale asked, studying their purchases.

"Sweaters and bonnets," Judy suggested. "It's cold today and they'll need them under their buntings."

"Irene and her friend have those. Gifts," Dale explained. "Pauline brought them. You remember Pauline Faulkner, of course?"

Judy nodded. She couldn't very well forget Dr. Faulkner's pretty dark-haired daughter for she and Irene had been visiting her when they met Dale Meredith.

"Well," Dale continued, "Pauline got acquainted with this other girl, too, and brought them each a sweater and bonnet set."

"Were the sweater and bonnet sets just alike?" Judy questioned.

"I wouldn't know about that," Dale said. "I told you I was no expert on baby clothes."

"I'm not either," laughed Judy. "I wish I were because it just occurred to me that perhaps Irene and her friend wouldn't want all the clothes alike. Suppose the babies got mixed up or something."

"That's impossible," Dale said with assurance. "You ought to know how particular they are in hospitals. Judy Irene's footprints were taken only a few minutes after she was born. Besides, all the babies wear little bracelets with their names in blue or pink beads, depending on whether they're boys or girls. There can't possibly be any mixup as the hospital gives them the bracelets and they wear them home."

"I suppose not," Judy agreed. "I've heard Dad say the same thing and yet he says that every mother has a secret dread of taking home someone else's child. All new babies do look something alike, you know."

"Irene wouldn't agree with you there. She thinks Judy Irene is the sweetest and prettiest baby alive."

They were at the accommodation desk waiting to have their packages wrapped as they talked. Now Dale tucked them under one arm and, with the other, escorted Judy to the car. It was parked quite a distance away as parking space is scarce in New York's great shopping area.

There was much to discuss as they walked to the car. Dale noticed Judy's ring and she told him of her engagement.

"So you finally made a choice," joked Dale. "For a while it was a toss-up between Peter and Arthur. I suppose Arthur is none too happy about it."

"On the contrary," Judy retorted, "he's

quite delighted about it. He and Lorraine Lee
were engaged first. That was exactly the way
we both wanted it. But I'm sure I wrote to
Irene and told her.''

"Perhaps you did and she neglected to tell
me. She's had so much on her mind. You
knew about her father's death?"

"Why, no!" Judy exclaimed in surprise. "I
knew he was worse again but no one told me
anything more. Poor Irene!"

"It was hard on her," Dale admitted. "She
collapsed right after his death and had to be
kept in bed for several weeks. But, thank
Heaven, she's all right now that the baby's here.
She's just as gay and lighthearted as she ever
was. She says you've been like a sister to her,
Judy. Both of us appreciate how much you've
done for us in the past. Never think we don't.''

That meant something, coming from Dale
who had so often criticized her.

"It's what I can do in the future that I'm
worrying about now," Judy said. "What
about the nursemaids I'm supposed to interview?"

"The emploment agency is our next stop,"
Dale told her. "Then lunch and then the hospital. How good it will seem to have my little
family home!"

"Is there anyone there to help if we don't get
a nursemaid?" asked Judy.

"Only a colored woman who does the cooking and cleaning," Dale answered. "But she has a family of her own and goes home at night. I'm afraid she won't be much help with the baby. You see, Irene wants a girl who will live with us as almost a member of the family. She has practically described her to me and no other girl will do. She must be young, attractive, likeable and yet as capable as an older woman. She must qualify as friend as well as nursemaid. I half expect Irene wants her for a companion as much as anything. She doesn't like being alone in the house."

Judy could easily understand that.

"I thought you might as well know what Irene expects of this nursemaid," Dale went on, "and why I called it a problem. She says to tell you that unless you like the girl yourself —like her as well as Lois or Lorraine or Honey——"

"Oh, but that's impossible!" Judy interrupted. "I couldn't like her as well as Honey. She's Peter's sister and, honestly Dale, I'm in love with his whole family."

"Or Selma or Scottie or, perhaps, Pauline Faulkner or Sylvia Weiss," Dale continued, undaunted.

"It's getting a little more probable," Judy admitted. "But naturally I couldn't like a stranger as well as I do my best friends."

"You like quite a lot of people, you know," Dale reminded her.

"I'm always getting myself involved in their affairs, if that's what you mean," laughed Judy. "Nearly every one of those girls you mentioned have been mixed up in a mystery or else helped me solve one. The latest was a little witch named Sally."

"Maybe we could mix this nursemaid into some mystery."

"I'd rather not, where Irene's baby is concerned," Judy replied, taking his suggestion more seriously than he had intended it. "But there is a mystery I'd like to solve while I'm here. When we have finished with the nursemaids I may tell you about it."

CHAPTER VI

THE EMPTY SETTING

Judy left the employment office much later feeling that she and Dale had wasted a great deal of time—both their own and that of the girls they had interviewed. If Irene hadn't been so particular Judy could have chosen a nursemaid from among them. One neat-appearing young woman impressed her as being efficient and responsible. But there was nothing charming about her. Judy couldn't honestly expect Irene to take her to her heart as a friend. The others were hopeless.

"It is discouraging," Judy admitted as they turned away. "How much simpler to be poor and look after your baby yourself."

"We're not rich," protested Dale. "Heaven forbid! But Irene isn't strong. She worked too hard when she was little, as you know. Besides, she's anxious to keep up her radio work. With her voice, it would be a shame not to."

"I know," Judy said. "Forgive me for being facetious. I'm the same way. I won't want to give up solving mysteries either. But then," she added cheerfully, "I probably never will—with Peter for a husband."

"You're a lucky girl."

"What about you?" Judy challenged him. "You just don't know how lucky you are. There isn't one girl in a million as sweet as Irene. And soon I'll be seeing her! Dale, why can't we *hurry*? Do we have to eat lunch?"

"I know a place where all the orders are rush orders—and then to the hospital. You'll have to be nursemaid, Judy, until we find one."

Judy smiled raptly. She would love that. As a little girl, she had always longed to have a baby brother or sister to tend. She hadn't cared much for dolls because they weren't alive. But her doll clothes had been used often, either for dressing up her kittens or for outfitting the ducks and chickens on her grandmother's farm. Once, to that old lady's horror, she had even dressed up a pig. But never a real baby. She felt, as they neared the hospital, that one of her dearest dreams was close to fulfillment.

Judy's impatience brought them to the hospital ahead of the scheduled time and, since men were not admitted above the first floor except during visiting hours, Dale was obliged to wait in the reception room downstairs. But Judy, to her profound joy, was allowed to go up. She was breathless from hurrying up the hospital stairs when she first glimpsed Irene.

Dale called her his golden girl, but now she was more golden than ever with her hair loose about her face. She was not yet attired in her street clothes but wore a pale blue satin robe that made her look like a princess. Judy had to stand a minute and stare at her.

"Judy!" Irene exclaimed the moment she saw her. "I'm so glad you came. I can't tell you how much I need you." Then Irene turned to the other bed. There were two of them in the room and beside the other one a girl sat reading a magazine. She had light brown, fluffy hair and wide, rather wistful blue eyes. She looked scarcely twenty.

"Jane, this is Judy—the girl I've told you so much about. Now do you see why I named my baby after her?"

Jane looked up, studied Judy's face a moment as though in approval and then smiled.

"Indeed I do. I'm glad to know you, Judy. Or should I say 'Miss Bolton?'"

"I should have said Mrs. Merrit," Irene apologized. "But I never do get introductions straight. It annoys Dale dreadfully."

"Cheer up," Jane laughed. "He isn't here to be annoyed."

"Anyway," Irene added, "we're only girls, even if two of us do have babies. It hasn't made us seem much older, has it?" she finished a little anxiously.

"Younger, if anything," Judy said—and meant it.

She tossed her load of packages onto one of the vacant beds.

"Here are the baby clothes. Dale and I shopped for them this morning. We bought two of everything. I hope you don't mind."

"Mind!" Irene exclaimed, throwing open a box and holding up one of the little dresses for Jane to see. "Why should we *mind?* It will be such fun dressing them like twins! They were born on the same day, you know. That does make them twin friends."

"That's one of Irene's notions," Jane said, "bringing them up to be friends because we are."

"You really are very good friends, aren't you?" smiled Judy, looking from one of them to the other.

"You'd think so," Irene returned, "if you could have been here with us. We never had such a good time. After the first day we felt so well that we had to think up games to amuse each other. We played ghosts. Do you remember it, Judy?"

"I think so. It's something about finishing words, isn't it? You think of a word and spell the first letter and keep on, back and forth, until you've finished it."

"And if you can't do it you're a ghost."

"No, only a *g*," Jane corrected her. "You have to miss five times before you're all five letters g-h-o-s-t."

"You ought to know," laughed Irene. "You didn't know how to spell *raisins*."

Jane giggled.

"You can guess who was ghost most of the time, can't you?"

Irene was dressing as they chattered. She looked like a school girl in the simple blue dress she slipped over her golden head. Jane was ready and waiting in her clean, though somewhat shabby, blue serge suit.

"We're both going home today," Irene explained. "But Jane's husband is out of town so she's riding along with us. I have her name and address and the apartment house telephone number in my purse so that we can get in touch with each other again. It will be nice to go home together. Dale won't mind taking Jane, I'm sure. It isn't out of the way."

For the first time since Judy had met her, a cloud crossed Jane's pretty face.

"I'm a little suspicious of husbands who 'don't mind.' Usually they do."

"She hasn't been as lucky with her husband as I have been with mine," Irene explained. "They don't get on."

"You put it mildly," Jane said. "We fight like cat and dog. I've had such a good time here in the hospital, I may as well confess it, I almost dread going home. Take my advice, Judy, and don't get married.''

Judy glanced at the ring sparkling on her finger. She had meant to tell Irene about her engagement. But Irene hadn't noticed the ring and, after Jane's remark, Judy thought it best to wait until they were alone to tell her.

''All husbands aren't like yours, Jane,'' she said, defending them. ''Look at Dale and Irene. They're happy.''

''They think they are——''

Jane broke off, her eyes lighting up as Irene suddenly exclaimed, ''Look! The nurses are bringing in the babies. The *lambs!* Now Judy can help us dress them.''

The nurse appeared at that moment, looking quite stern. Instead of a baby, she held a blanket which she promptly spread upon the bed. Then she faced Irene.

''You girls are a little too active for convalescents,'' she stated. ''Too much excitement may do you harm. Now just sit down, relax a little and I'll bring the babies in. Your friend can help you dress them. Is your husband downstairs, Mrs. Meredith?''

Irene nodded.

''He may come up now. And yours?'' She turned to Jane.

''I'm going with them.''

Jane's thumb indicated Irene and included Judy and the absent Dale. Judy offered to go down and tell him.

Downstairs she found him at the desk paying bills and signing certain things that needed to be signed. All this took quite a little time. But finally he turned to her.

"Well, am I admitted into the sanctum sanctorum?"

"You are. It's two o'clock. We were early," Judy explained, "and we would have had to wait anyway because Irene wasn't ready. But now she is. Ready and eager to be off. Jane's coming too. You don't mind?"

"Of course not. I think it's great that she and Irene are such friends. What do you think of her, Judy?"

"She's charming. You know, Dale," she went on enthusiastically, "I always used to think mothers were grown up. But if Jane is grown up—and Irene. They're two of a kind. But *so* delightful. They make me feel positively old."

"You are older than Irene in a great many ways," Dale answered seriously. "You see, while you were being a child, Irene was a grown-up, responsible girl looking after her crippled father. She's entitled to a little fun now, don't you think? I wouldn't want her to take motherhood too seriously."

"Don't worry. She doesn't. I haven't seen the lambs, as she and Jane call them. But they'll be there by now. Come on up."

"Do you mean," Dale asked, looking at Judy as though he believed such a thing incredible, "that I am actually going to hold my daughter instead of peering at her through a glass?"

"Come and see," coaxed Judy.

Dale needed no coaxing. Together they mounted the stairs but, at the door, stood speechless. Irene was bending over little Judy, dressing her, and on her face was such an expression of love and beatitude that Dale could only whisper, "The Madonna," and tiptoe in.

"Look at her!" Irene exclaimed as he came closer. "Isn't she heavenly? I've never seen her in anything but hospital clothes before."

Somehow, she reminded Judy of a little girl dressing a new doll. And, indeed, Judy Irene was doll-like in her delicate beauty. Her hair, what there was of it, was golden blonde and her cheeks were the pink of rose petals. She was wearing the dress with the pink feather-stitching and her tiny hands just showed at the end of the sleeves.

"I put it on her myself," Irene continued fondly. "Forgive me, Judy. The nurse said you should do it. But I couldn't wait."

"Of course you couldn't," Judy murmured in understanding.

"Put on her bunting," Irene directed. "See how adorable she is in it. I'd call her Rosebud if I hadn't already named her Judy. What's the matter? Can't you do the buttons?"

"I'm a little trembly, I guess," Judy admitted. "Silly, isn't it? But I'll manage."

Across the room Jane, alone now, was slowly and laboriously pulling the other dress with the pink feather-stitching over her baby's head. Judy felt suddenly sorry for her, having no one to share the adventure of going home.

"I'll help Jane," she offered, and felt amply repaid for her thoughtfulness by the look of gratitude that flashed across the other girl's face.

When the babies were all dressed—sweaters, bonnets and all—and buttoned into their buntings, the two mothers surveyed them proudly.

"Look! They're just alike."

And indeed they were. Two tiny pink faces, two pair of tightly closed eyes and two buntings that nearly enveloped them.

Dale was about to take Judy Irene in his arms when a nurse intervened.

"We carry them as far as the reception room," she said. "After that they are your responsibility."

The babies were carried down—first Judy and then Jane, for Jane had named her baby after herself. They would have been taken directly to the car but Irene had forgotten something. It was a plant someone at the broadcasting station had given her and she wanted to take it home, so Judy ran up after it while Dale, Irene, Jane and the two babies waited in the reception room.

The plant was a lovely little flowering primrose. Judy held it carefully and started downstairs with it but she had hardly gone half way when a man brushed rudely past her.

"Here! Here!" a nurse called frantically from the downstairs desk. "You can't go up there."

"But I want to see my wife——"

"You'll have to show your pass. No one is allowed above the first floor without a pass."

"Very well," said the man and descended meekly enough to fill out the blank that the nurse handed to him.

Judy returned with the plant, explained to Dale how one stem had been broken by a man who had hurried past her. Then, as she handed it to him, she happened to glance at her finger. She looked again, horror dawning slowly on her face.

"My stone!" she gasped. "It's gone! I've lost the diamond out of my engagement ring."

CHAPTER VII

WHILE THEY SEARCHED

IMMEDIATELY Dale was filled with concern. He had been waiting for Judy at the foot of the stairs, intending to carry the plant out to the car before returning for the girls and the babies. Naturally, he had seen the man who brushed against her.

"Careless pup!" he muttered. "Why doesn't he look where he's going?"

"He was in an awful hurry and probably didn't mean it," Judy said. "But he did knock my hand against the stair rail. I'm sure that must be when the diamond fell out of the setting. It happened when I was on about the fifth stair from the top. But the diamond may have fallen over the stair rail."

"Well then," Dale declared, "it must be either on the stairs or on the hall floor. It won't take but a minute to find it. Irene!" he called into the reception room. "We'll be a minute longer. Do you mind waiting with your precious daughter?"

"It will be a pleasure," Irene called back. "She and Jane will keep each other company," Dale remarked, turning to Judy, "and we'll hunt until we find your diamond. There's no need worrying them. It's sure to turn up since you know exactly where you lost it."

"Of course, I don't *know*," Judy said. "But I certainly think I lost it on the stairs."

"Do you have any pockets or anything where it might have been caught?"

Judy shook her clothing thoroughly. Nothing fell from it except her handkerchief and then she shook that.

No one, she observed, had gone up or down the stairs since the man had brushed against her and so no one could have possibly found the diamond.

"It must be here," she kept repeating to herself as she searched each separate stair.

But the more diligently she searched the more certain she became that the diamond was not anywhere on the stairs.

There were no cracks in either the stairs or the molding at the side. Everything was scrubbed clean. Not a speck of dust—not a speck of anything marred the whiteness of the hospital stairs. The black rubber stair cushions shone like newly shined shoes. So did the black and white linoleum in the hall below. There was no possible place to look now except between the stair rails. Judy searched them systematically, beginning at the top and looking behind each rail until she had reached the bottom, but without result. She was beginning to feel panicky. Suppose she didn't find the diamond! How could she ever tell Peter that she had lost the stone out of his grandmother's ring—the treasured engagement ring that he had given her?

Meanwhile Dale, who would have looked ridiculous if he hadn't been so in earnest, was spatting his hands over every inch of the downstairs hall.

The nurse at the desk grew curious. She stepped out of her glass cubicle and inquired unnecessarily, "Have you lost something?"

Dale looked up, faintly amused. Why else would he be crawling all over the hospital floor on his hands and knees? But Judy was too upset to see anything humorous about the situation. She answered tragically, "The diamond out of my ring," and showed the nurse the empty setting.

"But are you sure you lost it here?" she inquired.

"Quite sure," Judy returned. "It must have been when that young man bumped into me."

"I shouldn't wonder," sniffed the nurse. "Such a performance! I can tell you, I breathed much easier after he was gone."

"Did he find his wife?"

"She had already checked out. You know, we're not supposed to discuss the patients," the nurse informed her curtly. "Now, if you will wait a moment, I'll ask one of the internes to help you look for your diamond. Have you searched the room upstairs where you were visiting?"

"Not yet, but I had it then—" Judy began.

"You may have been mistaken. I'll call one of the nurses to help you."

The search now began in earnest, with nurses stripping the upstairs beds and internes flooding the entire stairway with light. Even the scrubwoman helped. There was pride in her voice as she announced, "They may find your diamond, dearie. But not a feather of dust will they find. Be gorra, not a feather!"

A wail from the reception room reminded Dale that it would soon be feeding time for the baby. Irene had given him a slip with the hours carefully checked off. She called to him now.

"Will you be much longer, dear?"

"Only a minute or two," he called back as cheerfully as though nothing had happened.

Judy was still trying to make herself believe that she would find her diamond.

"Did you look in the reception room?" one of the internes inquired.

"I wasn't in there."

"Then there's no use looking."

"No, I guess not," Judy agreed with a sigh as she turned toward the desk. "It looks as if we'd have to go home without the diamond," she said to the nurse.

"It's quite possible someone may find it after you're gone. Leave your name and address with me, also your telephone number," the nurse directed. "We will see that you are notified at once if the diamond is found."

Tears were very close to Judy's eyes at the sound of the *if*, but she gulped them back remembering that she was grown-up and couldn't cry right out in public.

"Thank you," she murmured. "I do hope you find it. It—it came out of my engagement ring."

"You poor girl!" There was genuine sympathy in the nurse's voice. Judy knew she would help if she could.

"The diamond must have been lost in the hospital," she told her. "I remember looking at it upstairs. I was going to tell the girls about my engagement and then decided not to. They hadn't noticed the ring. But it had the diamond in it then. I remember how it sparkled. I remember thinking, how could they not notice it. But, of course, they were so excited over taking the babies home."

"Naturally, they would be," the nurse answered understandingly. "Now, cheer up, for your friend's sake. Your diamond is quite likely to be found—if not today, then tomorrow when Mrs. Sheehan cleans. She's an honest woman and I'm sure you can depend on her to turn it in."

"Tell her there's a reward, won't you? May I post a notice on the bulletin board saying there's a reward?"

The nurse agreed to this and Judy wrote out the notice and tacked it up herself. It made her feel as though something had been done about it, at least. But she couldn't really believe that the diamond would be found. They had searched so thoroughly.

"Now, Mr. Meredith," the nurse said, turning to Dale who was still standing beside the desk. "You really must get your wife and baby home and she must rest. This is only the third day she's been up, you know."

"What'll we tell Irene?" Dale asked, turning to Judy.

"Why, the truth, of course," she answered. "What else could we tell her?"

"She mustn't be upset."

"I know that," Judy replied a little impatiently. "I won't cry about it, if that's what you're afraid of. I'll just tell her I lost it. That shouldn't upset her."

"It won't if you don't appear to be upset

yourself," Dale agreed and, taking her arm, they walked back into the reception room.

Judy expected to see Jane and Irene waiting there with their babies. She could tell them about the lost diamond, she thought, when they were in the car going home. But where was Jane? Irene, looking a little white and tired now, was sitting on a long sofa holding a baby. But Jane and the other baby were gone!

CHAPTER VIII

TOWER HOUSE

"Where's Jane?" Dale asked at once. "I thought she was riding home with us."

"She thought so too," Irene answered, "but her husband thought differently. He came in here like a whirlwind and hurried her off. It's too bad for I'm sure she didn't want to go. If you and Judy hadn't taken so long we might have missed him. Whatever were you doing?"

"Looking for something," Judy told her. "Irene, do you know whether or not Jane's husband started upstairs before he came in here?"

Irene shook her head. "I was reading a magazine and didn't pay much attention. But I know he came in here through the wrong entrance. It was that door."

Irene pointed and then Judy noticed another door which she felt sure must have had a table against it. But now the table was pushed away and the door stood partly open. Beyond it was a porch with a rail around it, but no steps. Irene's husband must have lifted her over the rail.

"Well," Judy said, forgetting to be cautious, "some blundering man brushed past me on the stairs and broke your plant and knocked the diamond out of my engagement ring."

"Judy!" Irene exclaimed in surprise. "You didn't tell me you were engaged. But what a pity to lose your diamond! Aren't you almost heartbroken?"

"Well, I feel badly about it, of course," Judy admitted. "But not as badly as though I'd lost the whole ring. After all, it's what it stands for that's important. I can wear it anyway."

"Not without the diamond. We must find it!"

"Now don't get excited about it, dear," Dale told her gently. "We've done everything we could and it will probably turn up in a day or two."

Judy suddenly had an idea.

"The nurse will know who that man was and we can ask him about it. She took his name. I saw her doing it."

At the desk Judy was not surprised to learn that the man who had bumped into her was Frank Merrit, husband of Jane. No wonder they didn't get on!

"But you told him she had checked out?"

"Quite true," the nurse agreed. "She had checked out. I had no idea she was waiting in the reception room. I suppose he may have seen her through the window and gone in through the blocked entrance. It was like him. Poor girl! I feel sorry for her taking a new born baby home to a man like that."

"I do too," Judy agreed, "and I do hope someone finds my diamond. If that man . . . But, of course, he couldn't have found it," she finished sensibly. "He ran up the stairs and then down and didn't even stop to pick anything up."

In the car going home Judy forced herself to be cheerful. She felt guilty, letting all this fuss about the ring spoil the day that had begun so beautifully for Irene. It must be a happy homecoming.

The primrose plant, looking as sorry as Judy felt, stood on the floor of the car. Judy wished now that she could have gone to Tower House first, arranged a plant or a vase of flowers, perhaps, or done something to make the place more cheerful. She remembered that Irene had been away two weeks.

"Is the baby's bed ready?" she asked, having no idea what preparations had been made.

Irene's face lighted up. "Oh, yes! It's so lovely. The nursery in the tower is fixed just as beautifully as my grandmother ever fixed it for my mother. You remember how my grandmother wrote:

'I'll enthrone you, my queen, in a cir-
cular tower
Where frost cannot blight my most
delicate flower.'

"I've always loved those lines best of all her
poetry and I'm enthroning Judy Irene just as
she did. But I hope," she added, "that I won't
ever love her quite as selfishly as my grandmother loved my mother."

"You won't. There isn't a selfish bone in
your body," Judy assured her warmly. She
knew that Irene was referring to the old romance of Tower House. But the whole tragic
story, uncovered when Judy solved the mystery
of the Yellow Phantom, never would have happened if Irene's grandmother hadn't been a little queer. "The crazy poet," her agent had
called her. But, "She just couldn't stand trouble," was the way Irene explained it. Whenever she spoke of it Dale gave her a look that
said, "You, my sweet, must never have any
trouble to stand."

Judy knew he had made this resolve and
liked the tender way he treated Irene. It was
best for Irene. But just the same she was glad
that Peter never thought of her as a delicate
flower. He did call her angel at times. But
she was sure his idea of an angel was not an

ethereal cherub with its elbows on a cloud. It was, rather, a noble person doing something good on earth.

"An angel," she thought, her lips tightening. "A fine angel he'll think me when he hears what's happened to his ring. He'll think I don't *care*."

Irene's hand closed over Judy's.

"You're worrying about what Peter will say, aren't you, dear?"

"A little—and about your nursemaid and things," Judy half-lied. "It seems to take a long time to drive home, doesn't it?"

Irene nodded.

"I'm so—so tired. I wish I could sleep like little Judy. She's forgotten it's past her feeding time."

"Does she have a bottle?"

"Yes. Her skin's delicate," Irene explained, "and so the doctor put her on powdered milk. You'll have to fix it for her. The formula is in my purse. Do you know anything about babies' formulas?"

Judy confessed to a total ignorance of the subject and by the time Irene had finished explaining Dale had stopped the car before the door of Tower House.

At first Judy thought they must be stopping somewhere else. The house, which had once been about the queerest in all the Parkville section—and Parkville is known for its queer houses—was now transformed. White strip shingles covered the once drab-looking siding. The window frames were painted a cheerful green and the lawn which had been so overgrown with weeds was now neatly trimmed and surrounded by a hedge. That wasn't all. Gravesend Avenue, which had always made Judy think of an avenue at the end of a graveyard, now bore the new name, MacDonald Avenue. The muddy side street where they had turned off the avenue was newly paved and the house next to Irene's was fixed over too. In fact, the whole section seemed to have blossomed into beauty.

"And once," Judy told herself unbelievingly, "I thought that Tower House was haunted."

As they entered the front hall she saw that Dale had thought of all the things she had wanted to do for Irene. The hall was no longer a hall, but an entrance to the living room where fresh flowers blossomed in the twin vases on the mantle and also in a bowl in the center of the large library table. Everything was neatly dusted and the house had none of that stifling closed-in air that had been so evident when Judy had entered it for the first time. But that, she remembered, was just after a funeral. Sarah Glenn, Irene's grandmother, had just

died. Now the house was filled with the living.
Its past behind it, it looked to the future—just
as Judy did. She found herself wondering
about the house where she and Peter would live
and hoping that it might be an old house with
memories and, perhaps, a mystery or two. She
hoped it would be a house where there had been
romance and tragedy and life and death as
there had been in Tower House.

"I love it here," she said, walking over and
spreading her hands before the fire Dale had
just finished lighting in the grate.

There, on her finger, was the ring with
the empty setting. Her finger showed right
through the place where a diamond had sparkled and shone only a few hours earlier. "You
like diamonds and if you like me . . ." Peter
had said, putting himself second and the diamond first. But Peter was first in Judy's
heart, and always would be.

"It isn't the diamond," Judy told herself.
"It's what it stands for."

But even then there was the picture before
her face of Peter being hurt because she had
lost it. He would say, "What's a diamond?"
But before he said it there would be that strick-
en look on his face. He had trusted her with a
keepsake and she had broken his trust. Not
that she had meant to, but if she had been more
careful . . .

She thought of the reckless man hurrying up the hospital stairs. It was his fault, she felt sure, because he had knocked her hand against the stair rail. Poor Jane, to have such a thoughtless man for a husband! The setting was empty, but still Judy would not take the ring off her finger. It still meant that she and Peter were engaged and would some day have a home like Dale's and Irene's. Most brides wanted new houses but Judy hoped, when she was a bride, that she would have a house that was like her ring—old and romantic, but not empty . . . not empty.

She blinked her eyes hard. It was fortunate that Dale called her just then, for again she was on the point of tears.

"Irene is going to lie down," he said. "I insisted upon it. Do you think you can undress Judy Irene and give her her bottle? You'll find everything in the nursery—bottles, an electric warmer, the powdered milk. You have the formula?"

"Yes, I have it. I'm sure that I can do everything," Judy replied, glad that she would be busy now. It would keep her from thinking of Peter and how she was ever going to tell him about the ring.

CHAPTER IX

A TRAGIC MISTAKE

J UDY took the primrose plant up to the nursery with her. She thought it might as well sit on the window sill in the sunny tower. Perhaps the sunshine would revive it. Dale followed, carrying the baby up the three flights to the tower room.

"Oh, how beautiful!" breathed Judy as she opened the door. "A princess couldn't have a nicer nursery. When did you fix it?"

"Weeks ago—before Irene's father died," Dale said. "It pleased him to watch us doing it. He used to chuckle over the pink draperies and say we were tempting fate and it would surely be a boy. But Irene wanted a girl because this had been her mother's nursery. I wouldn't have cared for myself. Well," he finished, holding the baby back to give her one last, fond look before leaving her with Judy, "Your mother got what she wanted, didn't she, lambikins? I swear she looks smaller than ever in this big bunting. Hurry and get her out of it before she's baked alive."

The door closed softly behind him and Judy

turned to the baby, thinking how wonderful it
was to be loved as she was. Wooly dogs, teddy
bears and dolls looked down at her from the
shelves in the nursery. All the charming books
that had belonged to Irene's mother had been
saved for her. But everything was like new, so
carefully had it been kept. The pictures on the
wall had all been repainted by a mural artist.
It was all like new and yet Judy fancied she
could almost hear the voice of that other
princess who had ruled in this same nursery.
"Golden girl" her mother had called her.
Irene was the second "golden girl." Would
this baby, with her golden hair and deep blue
eyes, be the third?

"Little Judy," Judy whispered tenderly,
hugging the wooly pink bunting against her
cheek.

The baby did seem tiny. After undoing one
button Judy was able to lift her out of the bunting like a little doll. She removed her bonnet.
She had thought there was a golden cast to
Judy Irene's hair but now it was simply light
brown. Perhaps she wouldn't be a "golden
girl" after all. Her hair might be almost any
color when she grew up—that is, any light
color. It couldn't very well be dark like Dale's.

Next came the sweater. Judy didn't intend
to do more than remove the sweater and see

that the baby was comfortably dry. She could nap in her little white dress.

"Now for your pink crib," she crooned, lifting the baby from the bathinette where she had undressed her. The baby was very hungry by now and made loud, sucking noises as she crammed her whole fist into her mouth. Judy glimpsed the pink bead bracelet on her arm and remembered how Dale had said all the babies wore them. It was really quite pretty, Judy thought. She'd look at it more closely when she had finished preparing the bottle.

The formula was amazingly simple. You simply dissolved the right quantity of powdered milk in the right amount of boiled water, poured it into the bottle and slipped on the nipple. Everything was sterilized and on a tray. Dale must have done it himself or else Beulah, the colored woman, knew more about babies than he thought she did.

"Ready, lambikins?" asked Judy, using Dale's expression.

The baby let go her fist and began to wail, although she was still too young to focus her eyes and couldn't have seen the bottle. Judy tested the milk on her arm, remembering at the last minute that she had seen nurses do this. Then she held the bottle so that the baby could drink it. She was too young to try and hold it with

her hands but, as she drank, she waved her
arms about and the beads on her bracelet made
a little clicking noise that seemed to please her.
They were square beads, strung loosely, and hit
against each other with every motion of her
arm. The letters on them were black.

ME, Judy read. Then up went the baby's
hand.

That was the beginning of Meredith, thought
Judy. She knew that only the baby's last name
would be printed on the bracelet.

MERR . . . Had they misspelled *Meredith*
at the hospital? Judy grasped the little hand
and held it so that she could see the letters
plainly. They were *MERRIT,* not *MERE-
DITH!*

"Jane's baby!" she gasped. "Heaven help
me! What shall I do?"

For what seemed hours she sat staring at the
baby as it sucked contentedly on its bottle. She
felt as incapable of movement as the dolls or
teddy bears that stared down from the nursery
shelves. This was Jane's baby she was tending.
No wonder its hair had seemed a different
color! No wonder its bunting had fitted so
loosely!

She thought of Jane. What would Jane do
when she discovered the name *MEREDITH* on
her baby's bracelet? Would she get in touch

with Irene? It would be such a shock to Irene —such a shock to both of them. Judy could hardly bear to think of it herself.

Dale, passing by in the hall, called out cheerfully, "Everything all right, Judy? Is the lamb asleep?"

Then Judy had to let him know.

"She's asleep, but everything's all *wrong*, Dale. Come in at once. I must tell you."

The door flew open with such force that one of the teddy bears tumbled off the nursery shelf. The baby, who was just dozing off after her bottle, woke up and began waving her arms about, clinking the beads on her bracelet.

"That's what she did before," Judy said in a stricken voice. "That's how I knew it. Dale, look at her bracelet! Do you see what we've done? We've brought home *the wrong baby!*"

Dale was suddenly silent and fierce. He looked like a thundercloud as he stood over the crib, his black brows drawn together, studying the bracelet. Judy knew how she had hurt him. Her three words, *the wrong baby* had sent his whole world of happiness tumbling about his head. But Irene shouldn't know. Somehow, they had to change the babies around again before she found out. This was what Judy gathered from his few brief words.

"That address," he said in a hoarse voice. "It's in her purse. Get it and we'll shoot over there now while she's asleep. She's dead tired. She won't wake up for at least an hour."

"But the babies! How are we going to change them back unless we take Judy—this one," Judy corrected herself. "Besides, we have to bring the right baby home."

"I know that! Get her into that bunting as fast as possible," Dale directed, "and for Pete's sake, don't let her cry."

Judy hardly knew how she would stop the baby from crying in case she wanted to cry. But, fortunately, she was fed and rested and that helped. She dozed again, even as Judy dressed her. She handled her swiftly but carefully and in almost no time she and Dale had her in the car.

"East Seventeenth Street," Judy read from the card she had found in Irene's purse. "It's a low number."

"Must be near Church Avenue; we'll find it in no time. Lord, I hope there isn't any trouble."

"As if there hadn't been," Judy wanted to say, but refrained from saying it out of sympathy for Dale.

She remembered Jane's husband and dreaded meeting him again. He wouldn't take the blame for the mistake. He'd be furious and probably blame Jane. How had it happened, Judy wondered. But in her mind she could almost see that blundering man who had knocked against her on the hospital stairs picking up the wrong baby. It was quite likely that Jane still didn't know there had been any mistake. Dale said they must hurry before she found out.

Judy was a little afraid for him as he raced to make the green light at Ocean Parkway and swung recklessly around the corner at Church. After all, they did have a baby in the car—even if it wasn't his. She glanced at it and noticed that its two round eyes were wide open now. She hadn't seen Judy Irene with her eyes wide open and couldn't help thinking this baby was just as lovely, if not lovelier, than her little namesake. But they were alike. Irene had held little Jane all the way home from the hospital, never once guessing that she wasn't Judy. If it hadn't been for the name on the bracelet Judy herself wouldn't have known. It was strange how important that little pink bead bracelet had suddenly become.

CHAPTER X

THE EMPTY APARTMENT

"WELL, this must be the place," Dale announced, stopping before a six-story apartment that looked exactly like dozens of other apartment buildings in the city. The apartment number wasn't on the card so Judy and Dale began looking for names on the bell plates.

"Merrit," Judy whispered hopefully to herself as she looked.

But the nearest thing to Merrit was Meyer and that couldn't be it. There was only one empty bell plate. That might be the one. Judy pushed the button hopefully.

"They might have just moved in, you know, and not have had time to put their name in the bell plate," she explained to Dale.

They waited, but no buzzer opened the door for them. No voice, calling through the phone hooked at the side, announced that anybody was in the apartment.

"It's number 40," Judy announced, reading from the bell plate. "We might go outside and look to see if there's an empty apartment on the fourth floor."

"How could we tell?"

"There'd be no curtains at the windows or something." Judy attempted a laugh. "I thought you were good at figuring out these things. The detectives in your stories never miss a clue."

"This is different. Well, let's look."

From the sidewalk they had a good view of the whole apartment building. There were curtains at every window on every floor except the fourth. Two windows on that floor were curtainless.

"But look!" Judy said. "The apartment isn't empty. There's somebody in there now. It's a woman and she's standing with her back toward the window. Let's ring the bell again."

They rang and once again they waited. Dale shifted the baby from one arm to the other and then they waited some more. The place was as still as though it were uninhabited. Didn't any of the occupants ever sing or turn on the radio or make any noise? Didn't babies ever cry? Little Jane answered that question by beginning a sort of song. You couldn't call it quite a cry. It sounded like, "La-a, la-a, a-la!" Judy didn't know that nearly all new babies cry that way to exercise their lungs. She felt sure something was hurting it. While she was feeling for unfastened pins a tenant came in and opened the front door with a key.

"Mind if we go in too?" Dale asked. "We're looking for someone."

"Ring the bell then," the tenant replied shortly.

"We did," Judy told him, "but no one answered. Maybe you could tell us. Does anyone named Merrit live here?"

"Never heard the name. Try the superintendent." And the door slammed.

Judy sighed deeply.

"Sociable chap, wasn't he? But we could try the superintendent. Why didn't we think of it before?"

"Darned if I know." And Dale pushed the superintendent's bell.

After another wait a woman appeared and announced that she was the superintendent's wife. The apartment with the vacant bell plate, she explained, was unoccupied. Would they like to rent it?

"Is it that apartment with the front windows facing the street?" Judy asked.

"That's it. Nice view. You can see right across the Parade Grounds and Prospect Park."

But Judy was not interested in the view.

"Are you sure it's vacant?" she persisted. "We saw a woman with her back to the window——"

"I was up there myself only a moment ago,"

the superintendent's wife explained. "You see, the apartment isn't exactly what you call vacant. But it's unoccupied, if you see what I mean."

Judy didn't see and asked the woman to explain herself.

"Well," she went on, "a young woman came awhile back and paid something down on it and asked to store some things there. But she's never paid a cent since and, what's more, she hasn't come back. You can see for yourself that I only lose money on an empty apartment. So I was just up there trying to figure out where we'd store the things she'd left so's we could rent the apartment. I'll have them stored in the basement if you're interested in taking it yourselves. We have no objections to babies. The house is almost too quiet sometimes, I think."

Judy agreed with her, but she did not say so.

"We weren't interested in renting the apartment for ourselves," she explained. "But this woman who rented it may be a friend of ours. Did she leave any name?"

"No. Just paid me five dollars down on the apartment, moved in some things and I ain't seen her since. That was three months ago, but I'm still holding the apartment hoping she'll come back for her things and pay the back rent."

"Hold it awhile longer for her, won't you? Perhaps this will help." And Dale gave the woman a twenty dollar bill.

"Thanks! That'll help——"

"And you can help us," Dale put in quickly. "You see, this friend of ours seems to be missing and it's very important that we find her."

"Thank you again, sir," said the superintendent's wife. "I'll do what I can. Cute baby you got there. Ain't very old, is it?"

"Two weeks."

"Land sakes!" exclaimed the woman. "And out already! Ben't you afraid it'll take cold?"

"It might at that," Judy agreed, looking at the baby anxiously. She felt so helpless, knowing so little about babies. "Let's hurry home with it," she urged Dale.

Judy glanced back at the apartment after they had crossed the street to their parked car. She clutched Dale's sleeve and spoke in a whisper.

"She's still there, Dale."

He turned impatiently. "Who's still there?"

"That woman in the fourth floor apartment. She's still there with her back to the window."

"Well, what of it?"

"She couldn't be the superintendent's wife. The superintendent's wife couldn't have gone up there that quickly."

"She could in an elevator."

"But she wouldn't stand in that same position, with her back to the window."

"Maybe she would. There isn't time to argue about it now anyway," Dale said as he opened the car door, slid behind the wheel and handed Judy the baby.

"What are we going to do with her?" Judy asked as Dale swung the car out of its parking space.

"Take her home," Dale said dully. "There's nothing else to do with her. We can't leave her on somebody's doorstep."

Further than that, Dale seemed to have no plan. But Judy had. She intended to slip away again, the first moment she could, and go back to that empty apartment. She intended to see if it really was empty. And if it wasn't, then she meant to see what was in it. She'd find a way, even if she had to climb up the fire escape and break a window. There was something uncanny about that motionless woman. And the more she puzzled over it the more certain she became that it couldn't have been the superintendent's wife. She was rather broad across the hips while this woman at the window had been slim and stylish. Besides, they had been wearing different clothes.

Could it have been Jane, Judy wondered. Then why didn't she answer the bell?

The bell could have been broken. Jane could have been hiding from someone—but certainly not from either Dale or Judy unless . . . unless she had taken the wrong baby on purpose. But what earthly reason could she have had for doing that?

These and many other questions perplexed Judy but she said nothing to Dale. She didn't even ask how they were going to explain the mistake to Irene. Dale scowled so fiercely at the steering wheel that she didn't dare.

The baby kept up its continuous, "La-a, la-a, a-la," and the sound grew into more of a wail as they approached Tower House. To Judy's dismay, Irene was at the door.

"Dale!" she cried out. "Wherever have you been with my baby? I hadn't missed her until I saw you and Judy coming up the walk, but if I had, I think it would have frightened me almost to death. You ought to know more than to take her out the first day she's home from the hospital. Such a stupid Daddy! Give her to me at once. There, there, mother's precious lamb; it's all right now. You're home again."

And, without waiting for a word in explanation, Irene bore the baby indignantly away.

CHAPTER XI

DALE GIVES A COMMAND

DALE and Judy looked at each other blankly.

"She doesn't know," Judy whispered. "Irene doesn't know that little Jane isn't her very own baby."

"She needn't ever know," declared Dale, striding through the living room after Irene. Judy followed, frightened and curious.

"Here, give her to me. You're not strong enough to carry her upstairs." Dale's voice was more harsh than he realized. "Judy and I will take care of her. Come on, Judy!"

"Why, Dale!" gasped Irene, almost dropping the baby into his arms. "You never spoke to me that way before."

"Sorry, honey." He kissed her quickly and then almost ran up the stairs. Judy found it hard to keep up with him. In the nursery he flung open a drawer and produced a very vicious-looking pair of scissors.

"Get that bunting off her," he ordered. "Give me her arm. If we can't find the right baby we'll destroy the evidence." And, with that he cut the bracelet—*snip!* Right in two.

Judy just managed to catch it in time to keep it from falling apart. She tied the cut strings with hands that shook like an old lady's. She was thoroughly frightened now.

"Now hide it!" Dale directed. "Hide it where nobody will ever find it. And don't let me hear you breathe a word of this to a living soul. There's no need of spoiling all our lives just because you and I were stupid enough to outfit two new born babies just alike. Now, if we never locate Jane, Irene will still have her baby."

"But we must locate her——"

"That is of secondary importance," Dale interrupted. "Irene's happiness comes first. You know her family. Her mother died before she was twenty. Her grandmother—well, you know how she was. Nothing like that is going to happen to Irene!"

"I understand," Judy said weakly. "But Dale——"

"There are no *buts*. There's no use talking about it either. From now on *this* baby is Judy Irene. We'll do what we can to find the other baby, *but Irene mustn't know!*"

Judy couldn't have spoken after that, even if she had wanted to. The day had been too full for her to even think, much less discuss anything. Besides, you couldn't reason with Dale. She could see that. Once he had made up his mind, wild horses couldn't drag an idea out of his head. Peter wasn't like that, she thought thankfully. Peter would have gone back with her and they would have investigated that woman with her back toward the window. Peter wouldn't have asked her to keep any such terrible secret as this. There wasn't anyone in her family who would have asked such a thing —rather, commanded such a thing for Judy knew that Dale had given a clear command.

The baby was still wailing and the wind, outside the tower windows, seemed to have taken up its wail. Perhaps Judy was right after all and Tower House was haunted—haunted with fears and suspicions and secrets that were worse than ghosts. She shivered at the thought. How she longed to be home with her family, and with Peter who would understand if only she dared tell him.

"It isn't fair of Dale," Judy thought fiercely. "I can't stay here and pretend to Irene. . . . Oh, it's terribly, terribly unfair!"

Judy's suitcases were outside in the hallway, still unpacked. She was tempted to snatch them up and start home at once without any explanation. But if she did that, who would find Jane and the real Judy Irene? Dale wouldn't. He wouldn't go about it in the right way. He was used to solving mysteries on paper, not in real life. And when they found her, who would explain things then? Oh, it was such a muddle! Judy's head was in a whirl.

"If I hadn't lost the diamond out of my ring none of this would have happened," she thought miserably, clutching the bracelet.

The hard, square beads in her hand reminded her that she must hide it—quickly, before Irene found her with it. She glanced about the room. Where? Where?

Oh, for a secret panel, a loose floor board, even a knothole. But there was nothing except . . . She had it . . . the primrose plant! She would bury the bracelet underneath the roots of the plant.

She found a spoon. There wasn't time to look for a trowel. Digging the spoon handle deep into the rich soil that surrounded the roots of the plant, she made a hole and dropped in the bracelet. Just then a voice interrupted her.

"Judy Bolton! What are you doing? You've spilled the dirt from that plant on the nice clean floor of the nursery!"

Judy whirled about to face Irene. Her face grew crimson to her hair roots. Usually quick to think of an answer, this time she was unable to say a word.

"What has come over you? You're not yourself and neither is Dale. You do the strangest things."

And while Irene was talking in that hurt,

perplexed tone a voice inside Judy seemed to be repeating what Dale had commanded, "Irene mustn't know!" What was Judy to do? If she stayed, she must obey him. Already Irene was growing suspicious.

"I guess you'd do strange things too," Judy finally managed to say, "if you'd lost a diamond that meant—that meant everything. How was I to know it hadn't fallen in that plant—until I looked? I had the plant in my hands when I lost my diamond——"

This fact had just dawned upon Judy, but it sounded convincing to Irene.

"Of course," she agreed, looking as if a great load had fallen from her shoulders. "Why didn't we think of the plant before? And that's where you went with Dale, wasn't it? Back to the hospital to see if they had found it. But you should have told me. Dale always tells me things."

Judy turned her face away. She couldn't look in Irene's clear, trusting blue eyes after that. And suddenly she knew that she hated husbands—all husbands. She hated Jane's husband who had brushed so rudely past her and then hurried off with Jane, not waiting to make sure which baby they were taking. She knew, intuitively, that it had been Jane's husband who had snatched up the wrong baby. And she hated Dale because Irene trusted him when he expected to live a lie for the rest of his life if necessary. She might even hate Peter, once he was her husband. But she doubted that, even in her present hysterical state of mind.

Irene's voice came to her as though from a great distance.

"I guess you want to be alone, Judy. It's all right. I understand. The room next to this one is yours."

"Thanks, Irene," Judy murmured and actually managed to smile.

But, once in her room, she buried her head in her pillows and sobbed out all the despair that was in her heart.

CHAPTER XII

JUDY MAKES AN EXCUSE

THE sun shone brighter after the rain. In the morning Judy realized that she did have several clues and if she followed them carefully she was almost certain to locate Jane and the real Judy Irene. A mother and new-born baby didn't just drop out of sight. Jane's doctor, for one, would be pretty certain to know where she was. And there was the apartment and the things she had stored there. Judy might find a clue at the apartment—if she didn't find Jane herself. But the difficult part of it was, how could she get away?

"Dale can't go with me," she thought. "He can't leave Irene alone. Besides, he has his writing to do."

His office was at home but Judy couldn't think, to save her life, how he could put his mind on a story when his wife was tending someone else's baby and his own was—he didn't know where.

As she passed his room on the way downstairs it almost made her angry to hear the furious tapping of the typewriter keys.

"Dale's writing as though he were inspired," Irene announced happily at the breakfast table. "He came in, drank a cup of black coffee and then started right in on a story. I'm afraid he's neglected his writing lately and I'm so glad he's back at work. Emily Grimshaw has been hounding him for a story. She says his public will be on his neck if he doesn't produce one soon."

Emily Grimshaw was the eccentric but lovable old lady who acted as Dale's literary agent. Pauline Faulkner worked in her office, helping her read and correct manuscripts.

"How's Pauline?" Judy asked. It had just occurred to her that she might visit Pauline as an excuse to leave the house.

"Oh, she's all right. As much in love with her work as ever. She'll never forget you, Judy, for if it hadn't been for you she wouldn't be working for Emily Grimshaw. But, just the same," Irene went on, "I think I have more to be thankful for. If it hadn't been for you I wouldn't be Mrs. Meredith."

"And," Judy thought bitterly, "if it hadn't been for me, you'd be tending your own baby instead of Jane's."

Aloud, she said, "How's the baby, Irene? I noticed that someone had brought her down from the nursery."

"That was Dale," she answered quickly. "I

asked him to. What did you think of her, Judy? Did she seem all right to you?"

Judy took a large bite out of the toast she had just buttered, avoiding Irene's eyes. The toast was an excuse for not answering Irene's question directly. She went on speaking.

"You know, Judy, after you and Dale took her out yesterday she seemed a little different, somehow. More fretful, I mean. I weighed her this morning to see if her food is agreeing with her and she's lost eight whole ounces. I know babies are supposed to lose a little, but not eight ounces. I thought of calling up my doctor."

"I wouldn't," Judy advised. "Doctors don't like to be bothered with little things like that."

"I suppose you ought to know," Irene agreed, "being a doctor's daughter. But what do you think I ought to do?"

"Wait a week." Judy's voice was steadier now. "If she's still losing, after a week, that's time enough to call the doctor."

And, under her breath, Judy said a little prayer that, when the week was up, Irene would have her own baby. Judy Irene was probably all of eight ounces heavier than little Jane.

Irene looked thoughtful. Then she had another idea.

"We really ought to do something about getting a nursemaid, though. I won't be able to manage at all after you go home. You know, I want to keep up my radio work and how can I ever leave Judy Irene unless we have a competent nursemaid?"

"We'll see about finding one for you tomorrow," Judy promised. "I had something else I wanted to do today."

"Unpack?"

"I did that early this morning. I wanted to go somewhere if you don't mind too much."

"And leave me alone? Oh, Judy!"

"Dale will be here—" Judy began.

"But you don't know him when he's deep in a story," Irene protested. "He isn't here at all, really. His mind is off in the south seas or wherever it is that his story is happening. He grabs cold things to eat and rushes back to his work. Of course, I don't mind. It's thrilling to be married to an author. But it's a little trying too. You won't run off just now, will you, Judy?"

"Oh, not this morning," Judy answered lightly although she had hoped to spend the morning "snooping" as she called it to herself, around the empty apartment.

While they were preparing the baby's bottle Irene asked suddenly, "Judy, where was it that you wanted to go?"

"Dozens of places," Judy answered truthfully. "I'd thought of making a list of them. I'm all out of clothes and want to do some shopping and I want to visit Sylvia Weiss and Pauline Faulkner——"

"Why not ask Pauline here?" Irene suggested. "We could have tea together this afternoon. Beulah won't mind fixing a few sandwiches."

"I'll call her up," Judy volunteered. But she waited until Irene was busy with the baby to make her call. Irene musn't hear it.

"Hello. Pauline? This is Judy. Yes, I'm in town. Got in yesterday." Was it only yesterday, she thought, that she and Dale shopped for baby clothes and bought two of everything? If she could only tell Pauline! Pauline had helped her solve a mystery before. She might help this time. She must help, Judy decided, even though she couldn't tell her.

"Yes," Judy went on speaking into the phone. "I'm staying with Dale and Irene. Of course I think the baby's lovely. Who wouldn't?" They were lovely, both of them, she thought.

"Listen, Pauline," she managed to say at last, "Irene wants you to come over to tea. Can you get away from the office this afternoon and be here about two o'clock?"

"I think so," Pauline answered. "I'll try.

But two o'clock's a little early for tea, isn't it? Does it have to be today?"

"I must see you," Judy said, lowering her voice. "I have to get away from the house and if you are here you—well, you could send me on some errand or something, couldn't you? Or you could have something quite personal to discuss with Irene. Anything. I don't care what it is. But I have to get away."

"I understand," Pauline answered. "I know you, Judy Bolton. Don't think I'll ever forget the time you visited me and nearly drove me wild. You're mixed up in a mystery. I might have known you would be. You'll have to tell me about it afterwards."

"I will—afterwards." Surely, Dale wouldn't expect her to keep it a secret after the right baby was found. She could keep that promise if . . . if . . .

"You'll surely come?" she asked.

"I'll be there without fail at two o'clock," Pauline promised.

Judy hung up the receiver and went to her room to try and figure out what she could do with the few precious moments Pauline expected to give her. She must locate Jane as quickly as possible. Should she go back to the apartment and try and persuade the superintendent's wife to show her what was stored there? If it happened to be nothing but furniture she might waste a great deal of time and not find a clue to Jane's real whereabouts.

Perhaps it would be better to go back to the hospital and find out the name of Irene's doctor or the address her husband had filled in on that card at the desk. Judy had seen the cards when Dale filled in his. There was a place for writing the *present home address*. Surely Jane's husband couldn't have filled in the apartment house as Jane's present home address unless she actually lived there.

"I ought to map out a plan of action," she decided and opened her pocketbook to map it out in the little notebook she always kept there. Beside the notebook was another book—the lost bankbook Judy had meant to return to its owner. It had seemed like an important clue to rather an exciting mystery when she first started for New York but since then other, more exciting things had crowded it completely out of her mind.

"How foolish of me!" she scolded herself. "Here I've been searching all over for excuses and I have the finest excuse in the world right here in my pocketbook. A mystery that I can talk about! Irene will understand a lot of things if she thinks I'm solving a mystery."

With the bankbook in her hand, Judy hurried down the stairs.

"Irene," she asked, discovering her on the

living room sofa with the baby asleep in the carriage beside her, "are you still interested in mysteries?"

Irene looked up and smiled.

"I never liked them as much as you did. You look as if you'd just solved one. Tell me about it."

"I will. But I haven't solved it yet. I only hope to when I return this bankbook."

"Bankbook?" Irene questioned. "Whose is it? Let me see."

She was fully as interested as Judy had hoped she would be. The name, Ludwig Bull, sounded faintly familiar. She was sure it must be some prominent New Yorker.

Judy had to laugh at that. "Irene," she asked, "can you imagine a prominent New Yorker smashing through the window of our house in Farringdon because he was hungry and wanted a piece of pie?"

"My goodness, no," Irene replied. "I couldn't imagine it."

"I couldn't either. And I couldn't imagine a hungry thief having more than two thousand dollars in a savings bank. That's why I think he broke in because he wanted something else. And that," she finished, "is the mystery."

"You run into the queerest things."

"Don't I?" said Judy. And meant it.

"Well, what are you going to do about it?"

Irene asked after Judy had told her a few more details.

"I thought, if I returned the bankbook myself," Judy said, "I might meet the man who owns it and find out why he broke into our house. I might, you know, with a few clever questions."

"You certainly might."

"And I ought to return the bankbook as soon as possible."

"Of course." Understanding broke, like a light, over Irene's face. "So that was why you wanted to go out by yourself?"

Judy nodded. She felt a little guilty. Irene was so gullible. She had said so exactly what Judy had expected her to say.

"I don't really mind," she went on, "if it's a mystery. I know how you feel about solving things. You're really a born detective, you know, and I think it's a natural talent that should be encouraged—like Dale's writing or my singing. You could run over and see about it while Pauline is here this afternoon unless, of course, you wanted to visit."

"I do. But Pauline likes excitement. It will be nice to tell her what happens."

"Do it then. Let's look up this man's name in the phone book. I'm sure he'll have a telephone." And Irene ran to get the heavy Manhattan book. It wasn't there, so they tried Brooklyn.

Bull, Ludwig, attorney they found and wrote down the address.

"He's a lawyer!" Irene exclaimed. "Like Peter——"

"Not if he sneaks in a house at night without a good reason," Judy declared. "Peter wouldn't do that."

"And he lives right near the hospital," Irene went on excitedly. "Isn't that luck, Judy? You can stop in and see if anyone has found your diamond. You're not fooling me as much as you think you are. I can tell you're still unhappy about it."

"I am unhappy," Judy answered and it did her heart good to be saying something that was really true.

CHAPTER XIII

AMONG THE MISSING

JUDY was unhappy about a great deal more than her diamond. She wasn't used to deceiving. She hated making up excuses and pretending she was going out for one reason when she was really going out for quite another. Her conscience, inside her, seemed to be stabbing her with very real needles. And every time Irene petted and fondled Jane's baby it stabbed her afresh. Irene was growing fonder of the baby by the minute. Judy didn't quite see how anyone could solve that, even if Jane should be found.

She met Dale on the stairs at noon and his face was positively haggard. She didn't know whether to feel sorry or furious at him for spending the whole morning in his writing room.

"Do you have to write, today of all days?" she demanded. "A whole morning has been wasted when we might have been looking for——"

"Quiet, Judy!" he interrupted hoarsely. "Irene will hear you. Now won't you leave me alone? Aren't things bad enough without your scolding me for the only peace I have? I can forget this when I'm writing a story."

"Then I'm thankful I can't write. And I promise you, Dale Meredith, I'm not forgetting it for a single minute."

"Don't forget it, Judy," Dale said more quietly. "I'm counting on you to help. But please don't blame me for doing what I think is best. I love Irene. You must know that. And I believe my way is the right way—for her."

"It wouldn't be for me."

"I know it, Judy. But for Irene it is." And with that Dale passed on down the stairs to the kitchen where he found something cold to eat.

Fortunately, Irene was busy with the baby and didn't see him. But she saw the dishes he had left from his hurried snack and said to Judy, "It must be an awfully good story he's writing. He ate hardly anything and I told you how he is when he's inspired. I shall be anxious to read it when it's finished."

"So shall I," agreed Judy, wondering how it could be any sort of a story at all. "I may be able to give him an idea or two," she added, "that is, when I really get to working on this mystery."

"Why don't you go out now? You've had your lunch and I'll explain everything to Pauline when she comes in for tea. But promise you'll be back by five. She wouldn't want to miss seeing you."

"I promise," Judy said and meant to keep her word.

"Give my regards to Ludwig Bull, whoever he is," laughed Irene as Judy hurried out.

It took about a half an hour on the subway to reach the hospital. Judy had decided she would go there first. She was not surprised to hear that the diamond hadn't turned up although, the nurse said, everyone in the hospital had been searching for it.

"Was there something else?" she asked as Judy still hesitated at the desk.

Judy told her that there was. "I wondered if you could give me Mrs. Merrit's address. She asked us to call on her but—but it must have been the wrong address or something. The apartment where she was supposed to live is—well, it's empty."

"Was it just a social call you wanted to make?" inquired the nurse.

Judy thought of an answer quickly.

"Not exactly a social call. You see, I wanted to return something—something Mrs. Meredith borrowed by mistake."

It was true. Judy did want to return something. She wanted to return a baby. But the nurse couldn't know that, of course.

"In that case," she said, "I suppose we could make an exception to a rule and give out an address although, usually, any information our patients give us is held in strict confidence."

"I understand that," murmured Judy. But the nurse was already writing out an address on a plain slip of paper. It proved to be an entirely new address and not the Seventeenth Street number at all.

Judy studied it as she walked down the hospital steps. Then, recklessly, she hailed a taxi.

"I don't know where this is," she told the driver, showing him the slip of paper. "Will you take me there?"

"It's quite a distance, Lady. Out on the island."

"I don't mind. Hurry as fast as you can, won't you?"

"I'll hurry, Miss."

And soon Judy was bumping along in the back of the cab watching the meter as it climbed past the one dollar mark, then past the two. The street was beginning to look like a country highway.

"How much farther is it?" she asked at last.

"Only another mile or so. Not running out of money, are you?" The cab driver wasn't very polite.

"No. Only time," Judy said. "I'll never be back by five."

"I'll wait for you. Here's the place, Miss." And he stopped before a stone gate. There wasn't a house in sight.

"How do I get in?" Judy asked, gazing at the iron bars that blocked her way. The estate was protected as though from an attack. There were sharp spikes all along the top of the fence and when she pushed against it Judy found the gate was locked.

The cab driver watched with what she thought was amusement.

"Want me to toot the horn, Miss?"

"You might—" she began, but the horn which was really more of a siren interrupted her.

In another moment a man in uniform appeared at the gate and asked Judy whom she wanted to see.

"Mrs. Frank Merrit—if she lives here," Judy asked. Already she was beginning to doubt it. Jane's shabby suit certainly didn't look as though she lived on a Long Island estate.

"Mrs. Frank Merrit is not at home," the man told her.

"Then I'd like to see Mr. Merrit if I may."

"Mr. Frank Merrit is not at home either. Would you care to see Mr. Jordan Merrit? I believe he is at home and I am quite certain his wife will see you if the matter is important."

"It is. Very important," Judy assured him. "I have something I want to return."

She had learned, from her experience at the hospital that this was apt to be as good as a password. And so it proved. The man unlocked the gate and told her to follow him.

The lawn they crossed was big enough for a golf course. They passed a group of poplar trees and presently the house came in sight. It was even more magnificent than the Farringdon-Pett mansion in Judy's home town. But, unlike the turreted home of Lois and Arthur, this house was low-built with many wings and many chimneys. Judy had a feeling that she was stepping into it out of some dream. How beautiful it must be in the summer when all the shrubbery was gay with blossoms. Now it was a little drab for the trees around New York simply dropped their leaves. They didn't change glorious reds and golds as they did on the trees at home. There were a few crimson vines climbing up the stonework. But they were the only touch of color.

Judy pulled the knocker on the great door and a butler opened it. She tried not to stare. But butlers, to her, were people one saw in the movies, not in real life.

"Mrs. Merrit, please," she said in a faint voice.

"Whom shall I say is calling?"

"Judy Bolton, a friend of Jane Merrit's. I have something that belongs to Jane and I came to see about returning it."

The butler bowed and went out. The magic password had worked again. Presently she could hear clicking heels along the polished floor as someone approached. Her heart thumped half in fear and half in anticipation. Mrs. Merrit, a matronly lady in a dress that emphasized her poundage, seemed to fill the room with her commanding presence.

"Well, what is it?" she asked, looking at Judy as though she had no right to be there. And the worst of it was, Judy wasn't at all sure that she had.

"I have something that belongs to Jane Merrit," Judy stated, inwardly praying that the magic would still work. "I came to see about returning it."

"Jane Merrit is not at home," the older Mrs. Merrit said primly. "As a matter of fact, we do not expect her."

"Then won't you please tell me where she is?" begged Judy. "I must see her. It's very important."

"I'd gladly tell you where she is if I knew."

Judy let a little gasp escape her lips.

"You mean—you mean she's missing? Doesn't anybody know where she is?"

"Look here," said the woman, her attitude

suddenly changing, "if you're from the papers
I have already told them I am not giving out
any information."

"I'm not from the papers," Judy hastened
to explain. "I'm a friend. I met Jane Merrit
in the hospital and there is a mistake. We have
something that belongs to her."

"No doubt she needs it," Mrs. Merrit answered coldly. "She left here without a cent in
her purse and the Lord only knows who'll take
her in. She doesn't know a good home when
she has one. Why, there isn't a thing in the
world we couldn't give that baby. She could
be charged with criminal negligence taking
that poor little mite out in the cold. But there,
you're not interested in that, I'm sure. People
always tell me I talk too much."

"But I am interested," Judy protested. "If
you're trying to find Jane perhaps I can help
you."

"How, may I ask? The Missing Persons
Bureau can't find her."

"They haven't had time. When were they
notified?"

"Late last night. The city station broadcast
her description on the radio only two hours
ago."

Had Irene heard it, Judy wondered. She
could see no reason why Irene shouldn't know
that Jane was missing. That wouldn't be tell-

ing her about the babies. If she hadn't heard the radio broadcast Judy decided that she would tell her about it herself.

"I'm still waiting to hear just how you expect to be of any help," Mrs. Merrit said more sharply.

"I have several clues," Judy told her, "and I'm not altogether inexperienced in this sort of thing. The chief of police in my home town would recommend me, I'm sure. I've helped him on several occasions."

"And where, may I ask, is your home town?"

"Farringdon, Pennsylvania. It's about eight hours on the bus."

The woman gave a little start.

"And your name? Did I hear it correctly? Did you say it was Bolton?"

"That's right. My father is Doctor Bolton of Farringdon. Have you ever heard of him?"

"Never," replied Mrs. Merrit, her lips straightening into a thin line. "I think we can do very well without your help, Miss Bolton."

"But I want to help," Judy persisted. "You see, I have to find Jane because—because my friend, Mrs. Meredith, has something that belongs to her. And that isn't all. She has something equally important that belongs to Mrs. Meredith. I shall certainly do everything in my power to locate her."

"I think I begin to understand your interest," Mrs. Merrit said with a dry laugh. "I begin to see how our little Jane may not have been entirely without funds."

But Judy had never meant that. She had never intended to make the woman think it was money Jane had. She started to protest but then, on second thought, realized that since she couldn't explain about the babies, Mrs. Merrit might as well think what she would. She seemed more willing to talk now and told Judy a little more about her troubles with Jane before she left. From her story Judy was able to guess that Jane was simply an unwanted daughter-in-law in a rich man's family. She had left her husband as well as his parents and it was quite evident that she didn't wish to be found.

"That might explain the apartment," Judy said to herself as she walked down the long driveway to the gate. "That may be why she didn't answer the bell. She may have thought we were her husband's people."

The apartment, Judy decided, would be the very next place that she would call. She glanced at her wrist watch. No. She couldn't do it today. There was hardly time for her to keep her promise and be back at Tower House by five o'clock.

CHAPTER XIV

THE LADY IN THE WINDOW

PAULINE was just leaving when the taxicab pulled up before the house and Judy jumped out.

"Pauline! Pauline!" she called. "Wait a minute, Pauline!"

The girl turned and hurried back.

"You at last!" she exclaimed, embracing Judy. "Irene and I had just about given you up for lost. Really, dear, we thought something terrible had happened to you. Then we called up the hospital to find out if you had been there. Irene told me how you had lost your diamond and I'm so sorry. Well, they said you had and when we questioned them some more the nurse admitted that she had given you Jane's address and that you had immediately called a taxi. But why did you do that? Irene said you'd gone to call on someone named Ludwig Bull. That must be the mystery you were telling me about. The name itself would scare me out of my shoes."

"Oh, my goodness!" Judy said. "I forgot all about him. I've still got his bankbook."

110

"What did you do? You said you'd tell me."

"I will, Pauline. Only wait a minute. Let's go back in the house and tell Irene too. She's Jane's friend and ought to know about it. It was something quite unexpected."

"I can imagine," sighed Pauline. "Judy, you never grow a day older, do you? I can see you fifty years from now, a little old redheaded lady running about solving mysteries."

"What a horrible picture! I hope I shall be gray like other old ladies."

"You won't *be* gray. You'll just make other people that way."

Laughing, the two girls entered the house. Irene met them, looking white and worried.

"*I* don't think it's funny," she began in an offended voice. "Judy, what made you go out there? Jane wouldn't have liked it. She wouldn't have liked it at all."

Judy started back in surprise. How did Irene know where she had been? But she answered, just as though she had intended telling her all about it.

"You didn't hear the missing persons broadcast, did you? Well, if you had, you'd know why. Jane is missing. Naturally, I forgot all about the other mystery as soon as I heard it. Can you blame me, Irene?"

"I wish you'd asked me about it first," the golden-haired girl replied in a hurt tone. "I could have told you she never meant to go back to her husband's people. She told me all about that gilded cage out there on Long Island and how her husband's people watch every move she makes and treat her as though she weren't in her right senses. That may be the address her husband left at the hospital but her real address is in my pocketbook. It's an apartment on East Seventeenth Street. She's probably there this minute."

Judy thought of the curtainless windows and that strange, motionless figure with her back turned. She thought of the silence that hovered about the whole apartment building. "The house is almost too quiet," the superintendent's wife had said. And yet Irene was quite likely to be right. Jane and the baby might be hiding there.

"Did you see Jane's mother-in-law?" Irene interrupted Judy's thoughts to ask.

"Yes," Judy said. "I talked with her. I didn't like her."

"What was she like?" Pauline asked curiously.

"Oh, the type that likes to appear important. I can just see her in evening clothes showing off her buxom figure. The word "society" sticks out all over her. Really, she's quite awful. I imagine she winds her whole family around her little finger. She looks—well, a little like Mrs. Jiggs in the funny paper."

Irene giggled. "I thought she would. But Jane isn't the type to be dominated like her Mr. Jiggs and his weak-willed son. Jane says her husband is a much nicer person when he's away from his mother. But he likes to be pampered and he hates to work and so, naturally, he won't take on the responsibility of a home of their own. Jane has lost all respect for him because he's so weak."

"His manners are terrible," Judy said, remembering the encounter on the hospital stairs. "He certainly doesn't act as though he lived in a gilded cage, as you call it. But don't we sound like pussy cats, talking this way?"

"It isn't catty to be interested in our friends," Irene put in quickly. "And I am interested in Jane. I felt sorry for her. But she said she'd solve the whole problem and I shouldn't worry. That's why I'm not worrying about her being missing. She said she'd never go back and live with her husband's people."

"What else did she say?" Judy asked eagerly, realizing that she might learn more from Irene than from anyone else. "Did she have any money? How did she expect to take care of herself and the baby?"

"She had plans. Oh, she told me a lot! She'd saved some money and had it with her. The nurse kept it in the safe and then gave it back just before she was ready to leave. But I don't think she has it now. Her husband took it."

"How do you know that?" asked Judy. She was sitting on one side of Irene while Pauline sat on the other. Both girls' eyes were alight with interest—Pauline's because she loved a mystery and Judy's because she knew she had one on her hands and, while she loved them too, she was beginning to think this was a little too close to tragedy.

"Because," Irene answered, "when her husband came in I heard him say, 'I'm onto your tricks, Jane. Give me that pocketbook!' And then he snatched it out of her hands and she picked up the baby——"

"Oh!" gasped Judy. "She picked up the baby?"

"Of course. Why shouldn't she? She certainly wouldn't trust that blundering husband of hers to carry it."

"But where were you, Irene?"

"I had just walked over to the table to get a magazine. You and Dale took an awfully long time hunting for that diamond and Jane and I were both reading and the babies were sleeping there on the sofa."

"I see."

"Don't look so glum about it then? What was so terrible about that?"

Judy came out of her trance. She had been trying to see everything just as it had happened.

"Oh, nothing," she said. "Only afterwards Jane ran away with her baby. Her husband's people don't know where she is."

"Why should they?" Irene asked impatiently. "She had a right to run away with her own baby if she wanted to. She didn't want it brought up by that—that old dragon of a Mrs. Jiggs, I mean Merrit. Jane was thinking of the baby's welfare and I'm not worried about it at all. Jane will manage. She's not stupid. She's always managed before."

"How do you know she's always managed? What else did she tell you?" Judy asked.

"About how she left home at sixteen and Judy, I forgot to mention it, but I had met her before. We kept looking at each other there in the hospital and we didn't seem quite like strangers. Then I said, 'I've seen you before, haven't I?' Jane didn't think I had until I told her I used to work in the silk mill in Farringdon. She worked there too, when I first started in. But I've changed more than she has. She didn't recognize me."

"Then that woman did lie!" Judy said.

"What woman? Her mother-in-law?"

"Yes. Mrs. Jiggs-Jordan. She said she'd never heard of my father but she looked awfully guilty when she said it. I can usually tell when people are trying to hide things and, for some reason or other, she didn't want me to know she'd ever heard of my father. Strange, isn't it?" Judy asked.

"The whole thing grows stranger and stranger," Pauline agreed. "But now, for all I'd love to stay, I really must leave you. I have a date this evening with one of Miss Grimshaw's most promising young authors and I wouldn't miss it for the world."

"We understand," said Irene, smiling at Judy.

Pauline's interest in her work, they both saw, was not wholly in the manuscripts she read.

"Maybe some day we'll both be author's wives," Irene remarked after Pauline had left. "But, in spite of what Pauline says about Judy Irene's hair not being as golden as she thought it was, I'm sure nobody could have such a wonderful baby."

"Did Pauline say that? Did she look at—at Judy Irene very closely?" Judy asked, trying not to let her voice sound anxious.

"She looked at her all right," Irene answered. "The first thing she said was, 'How different she looks!' Dale heard her and he was furious. He's been working too hard and his nerves are all on edge. Sometimes I wonder if his stories are worth it."

"Maybe it would do him good to get away from that story for a little while," Judy suggested. "We might all go for a ride tomorrow and look up Jane at the apartment——"

"I wouldn't think of it!" Irene interrupted. "The baby's too young to be taken out visiting. You and Dale were very foolish to take her out the other time."

"I'm sorry about that," Judy murmured.

"Well, if you're really sorry, maybe you can think of some way to get Dale away from his story tonight. He mustn't be up there in his writing room all night again and Sylvia is coming in later. I won't be alone."

"Sylvia?" How well Judy remembered the dark-eyed little silhouette cutter. She would have loved to see her. But seeing what was in the apartment was more important.

"I'll get him away," Judy promised. "Maybe we could go to a movie——"

But Irene interrupted.

"No. Not a movie. That wouldn't be any rest for his eyes. Why don't you call on Jane by yourselves if you want to? Then Dale could drive you around to that Bull person's place to return the bankbook. You seem less curious about that mystery than I am. What has happened to Jane isn't really a mystery at all. Any girl would run away from such a husband and such in-laws. The only thing I can't understand is why she married him in the first place."

"He probably had a good line and Jane fell for it. That often happens," Judy said knowingly.

"You talk as if you were experienced," laughed Irene. "Just wait until you and Peter are married. Then you'll understand some of the difficult adjustments married people have to make."

"Am I so difficult?" asked Dale, appearing suddenly at the door.

Judy turned and, to her great relief, saw that he was smiling. He walked over and kissed Irene.

"I have been a bear, haven't I, honey?"

"I know. It's that old story," she sympathized. "But Judy and I have a plan to get you away from it. You're going together to call on Jane at the address she gave me. Her folks have given out the news that she's missing but I know better. Lend her a few dollars if she will accept it. I have a feeling she'll be needing money. And then," Irene continued, not noticing the look of concern on Dale's face, "drive around to another address that Judy will give you. She's found somebody's bankbook and it looks like quite a mystery. Let her tell you about it, won't you, Dale? You can't be puzzling over make-believe mysteries all the time. Maybe this one is just what you need to straighten out that plot that's worrying you so."

"I shouldn't wonder," Dale replied. "I see you girls have had tea. Have you thought about dinner?"

Irene was the picture of remorse.

"Oh, Dale! We didn't. We had no idea you'd be down to eat with us and we're not hungry. I told Beulah to wash up the tea things first but there's ham in the refrigerator."

"Ham and pie," said Judy, "and does that remind me of something!"

"Her mystery," Irene confided. "Get her to tell you about it, Dale. And if you're tired of ham, as I'm sure you must be, why don't you two run along and have a regular dinner in a restaurant? Judy hasn't been having cakes and sandwiches and tea all afternoon. She's been riding around in taxis. Get her to tell you about that too."

"I will," Dale said with a meaning glance at Judy. "All right, Detective, we're off to the apartment."

"Dinner first," Judy protested and made sure Irene heard her.

But once they were away from the house neither Dale nor Judy could have eaten a mouthful if they had tried.   Once more they were dashing around corners in the queer old Parkville section, racing to make the light at Ocean Parkway, turning at Church and finally swinging into East Seventeenth Street.   Judy glanced up at the fourth floor window of the apartment and then caught her breath in one long, horrified gasp.

The woman was still there.   She was standing before the window, as motionless as though she had been turned to stone.   Her white dress looked ghostly against the black window and Judy could see that she hadn't moved.   Jane's words came back to her, "You can guess who was ghost most of the time, can't you?"

Judy watched a moment longer.   Then she turned to Dale.

"There's no use standing here staring at the windows," she said.   "Let's go up."

CHAPTER XV

JUDY MEETS THE DETECTIVE

The apartment building was just as silent as it had been before—and more ominous. There was no answer when Dale rang the superintendent's bell. And there was no answer when he rang the bell to the empty apartment.

"Maybe, if we wait long enough, someone who lives here will let us in with a key," Judy suggested hopefully.

"Into the building, maybe. But that won't get us into the apartment."

"How about the fire escape?" Judy asked in a whisper.

"You could be arrested for that," Dale said grimly.

"Well, then, the police?"

This suggestion suited Dale better than the other. A missing person. A motionless form before a window. Surely it was reason enough for the police to issue a search warrant or rather, to force their way in without a warrant, as that was the procedure where a crime was believed to have been committed. But Judy didn't think so.

"We're really working with Jane's in-laws if we call in the police. They've already done that. Besides," Judy added, "I'd like to see a few things myself before a bunch of policemen began dusting everything for fingerprints. Things that looked like ghosts have turned out to be merely reflections or statues or goodness knows what. And we don't want to be laughed at."

"You're right there," Dale agreed. "What's your plan."

Judy rubbed her forehead thoughtfully with one gloved finger.

"Well, it's this way. I'm a friend of Jane's and Jane has something that belongs to a friend of mine. That's true enough, you know. And I came here to see if it was there. The superintendent wouldn't let me in so I climbed up the fire escape, for that, Dale Meredith, is exactly what I intend to do. You stay here and listen for the buzzer and I'll let you in properly through the door."

"I don't think you should, Judy."

"Neither do I," she laughed. "Now lift me up."

Dale, still protesting, did as he was told and Judy grasped the ladder at the end of the fire escape and began climbing like a monkey. She remembered that from the days when she used to climb the trees around her grandmother's place in Dry Brook Hollow. It was a little easier once she had reached the iron steps. She hugged the shadows for, just behind her, the windows were blazing with light. The fire escape was right at the front of the building and Judy knew she could easily be seen from the street if anyone should happen to pass by before she had reached the fourth floor window. She was almost there when a man, turning in at the entrance, observed her.

"Burglars?" he asked of Dale who was waiting for the buzzer. "Or did you just forget your key?"

"What do you think?" Dale asked, turning sharply and looking as annoyed as he felt.

The man chuckled. "Don't mind me, brother. I've often done it myself. But it's not necessary to break into this building. Come on up. I'll let you in with my key. Which apartment is it?"

"It's 4C!" Judy called down from the fire escape just above Dale's head.

The man gave a start. "Your echo, eh? Come down here, Miss!" he called more loudly. "That's no way for a respectable young lady to do. How did you think you'd get in once you were up there? Break a window? Or do you forget to lock your windows too?"

"I don't know—whether they're locked or not," Judy stammered, turning against her will and slowly descending the iron stairs.

"I see. You're the lady who moved her

things into 4C, aren't you? You *are* forgetful. You almost forgot to come back at all."

Judy's heart skipped a beat. Things were coming her way after all.

"He thinks I'm Jane," she told herself excitedly. "The babies are mixed up and now Jane and I are mixed up. What next?"

She remembered the little veil on top of her hat and hastily pulled it over her face so that, if the man had seen Jane, he might not notice the difference. A henna rinse, she thought, might account for the changed color of Jane's light brown hair.

Feeling that she had accomplished quite a clever transformation, Judy now dropped from the ladder at the end of the fire escape and landed on the solid ground below.

"That was a neat one. Good as a movie," chuckled the man who appeared to be an especially good-natured individual. "It looks as though it won't be so quiet around here with you folks moving in. Is this your husband, Mrs. Merrit?"

Judy shook her head. "No. Just a friend."

"Mrs. Merrit and her husband are separated," Dale stated, quite truthfully.

"And the baby? I heard there was a baby."

"A friend is keeping it for Mrs. Merrit."

So far, Judy thought thankfully, they had told the exact truth. And yet this man, who must be the superintendent, had been entirely misled. It all seemed very simple as he let them into the front door with his own key. But, once inside, he decided to make a phone call.

"Detective Murphy reporting," he said in a low voice over the wire.

Dale was about to protest but Judy motioned for him to be quiet. They both listened.

"I just caught a young lady who says she's Mrs. Merrit trying to break into the East Seventeenth Street apartment. What are your instructions?"

Judy couldn't hear the instructions but the detective said, "Okay!" And suddenly, Judy couldn't have told why, she burst out laughing.

"What a joke!" she laughed. "I didn't say I was Mrs. Merrit. You did."

"Take that veil off your face," ordered the detective a little less good-naturedly than before.

"Gladly," replied Judy. "You see, I'm not Mrs. Merrit. My name is Judy Bolton and I was doing a little detecting too. I thought there might be a clue or two in the apartment. But I suppose you've looked."

"And who are you?" the detective demanded, turning to Dale.

"My name's Dale Meredith."

"The detective story writer!" exclaimed Murphy, clasping his hand. "I've always won-

dered where you writer guys got your ideas.
Now I begin to see. Maybe we can do a little
work on this case together.''

Judy could have hugged the detective for
that. Nothing could have lifted Dale's de-
pressed spirits more than meeting one of his
fans. And it developed that Detective Murphy
had read practically everything Dale had ever
written.

''I suppose you'll make a story out of this if
we find the Merrit girl?'' he asked.

''Perhaps. But not just as it happened,''
Dale explained. ''A writer always has to cre-
ate his own characters. But I might use a situation or two.''

''For instance,'' Judy put in, suddenly inspired, ''he might use that woman in the window. You know, the one who stands there
without moving and looks like a ghost.''

The detective stared at her.

''I didn't see any woman in the window.''

''Well, she's there,'' Judy declared. ''It
may be too dark to see her now, but she's there
just the same. She hasn't moved since yesterday.''

''In that case,'' said the detective, ''we will
go up. All three of us. You're right. We may
find a clue, if not the whole solution to this
thing, in the apartment.''

The self-service elevator carried them
quickly to the fourth floor. Here all the halls

were bare. There was no sound except that of a radio, inside an apartment at the end of the hall. It was playing, appropriately, the *Danse Macabre*. The detective turned to Dale.

"Say, do you suppose we could bribe them to turn that thing off? Entering a vacant apartment like this, there's no telling *what* may turn up."

"Do you mean to say you haven't seen the apartment?" asked Judy. She couldn't imagine being assigned to investigate a missing person and not searching among the person's belongings for clues. But, apparently, the detective had just arrived at his post when Dale and Judy obliged him by trying to break into the very apartment he had been told to watch.

The radio played on. The piece began all over again just as Detective Murphy turned the key in the door of the empty apartment. It wasn't a radio at all, Judy decided. It was a phonograph with a repeater attachment. Atmosphere for their adventure! They stole in, tiptoeing to the strains of the ghostly music. Then Judy, who found the button first, flashed on the light and the spell was broken.

"Holy Moses!" the detective exclaimed. "It is a woman at that!"

And once again Judy, who had half suspected what it was from the very first, burst into a fit of laughter.

CHAPTER XVI

THE DETECTIVE MEETS THE LADY

"Detective Murphy," Judy called from beside the window, "come here and meet your lady. She's holding out her hand. I'm sure she's eager to meet all of us. I'm sure she thinks we're very brave, walking into an empty apartment and meeting a ghost, face to face. Come on. Don't be afraid. She can't hurt you. She's made of wax."

At that moment a mouse, who was probably the only living creature in the apartment up until then, fled from its nest and darted between the detective's feet. He spread them far apart, giving the creature plenty of room. Judy was next. The mouse ran straight toward her but Judy, instead of jumping up on a chair, simply stood there, still laughing. A little thing like a mouse couldn't frighten Judy. Blackberry dragged so many of them onto the porch at home that she was quite used to them. Alive or dead, they had no terrors for her. And, somehow, she didn't seem to be able to keep from laughing.

Outside, the phonograph—muffled now—still played the *Danse Macabre*. The detective's face was chalk-white and Judy was almost hysterical from laughing so much. As for Dale, he stood in one corner of the apartment like a man in a trance. The lady continued to smile at them with her wax lips partly open.

"What is this? A joke?" Detective Murphy managed to stammer at last. "I would have sworn that was a corpse when I first laid eyes on it."

"It's beautiful, don't you think?" asked Judy, her eyes still twinkling. After the suspense and heartache of the last two days it was good to find something she could really laugh at.

"Beautiful nothing!" spluttered the detective. "Look at those eyes! Glassy, I call them."

"Naturally," said Judy. "They're made of glass."

The detective stared long and thoughtfully at the lady in question. She was dressed in white organdie, a little dusty to be sure, but still white. Her hair was light brown like Jane's and she was about Jane's height and build. And she stood facing him, her back to the window. Finally he said, "Well, you tell me. Is this a woman or is it the wax museum?"

"I'd say it was a dummy out of a dress store window," Dale spoke up. "But what's it doing here?"

"Must I answer all the questions?" asked

Judy impishly. "It's stored here, of course. The missing Jane Merrit probably intended to rent a little shop somewhere and sell ladies' dresses. She has to make a living, you see, with a new-born baby to take care of. And this wax model looks quite realistic in her clothes, don't you think?"

The detective grunted.

"Realistic is hardly the word I'd use. Ghastly I call it."

"Her cheeks may have faded a little," Judy admitted, smiling at the detective. "But now that we've met the lady I suggest that we look about for other clues. After all, we were searching for Jane Merrit, not a dress model."

"You're right. Okay, Mr. Meredith," said the detective assuming a professional air. "Let's start searching."

Judy looked about the room. There were not many places where they could search. It was only a one room and kitchenette apartment to begin with and it was almost bare of furniture. A single bed with a cotton blanket stood in one corner. There were exactly three chairs and two of these were of the folding variety and went with a battered bridge table that leaned against the wall. A dresser with all the drawers empty and a writing desk had been pushed together in the center of the room and there was a shabby, rolled-up rug which the detective nearly tripped over. The wax lady, in her dusty organdie dress, completed the furnishings of the apartment.

Judy, still fascinated by her, was pirouetting around her examining her costume. It was a little long for present day styles, she thought. But it might have been a bridesmaid's outfit or a graduation dress. Underneath was a slip of purest satin and it shimmered through the folds of the dress.

"I think I'd call you Lady Elizabeth if you were mine," she whispered, making a curtsey to the lady.

She turned to see what effect that had on the detective but he wasn't watching her at all, only stealing stealthily toward the window. Judy noticed a darker shadow against the window shade and darted in ahead of him.

"Look!" she exclaimed, pulling aside the shade. "I could have climbed in from the fire escape at that. There's a broken place in the window right next to where it locks."

"Plague take me!" muttered Detective Murphy. "I thought it was a pixie fluttering against the pane."

"Pixies don't do that," Judy reproved him. "They dance, you know, on the dark side of the moon. And I think something bigger than a pixie came through that window."

"Wait a minute," cautioned the detective.

"Now here's something I can do. You see those fingerprints?" And he pointed out a few cloudy marks against the glass.

Judy laughed. "I know. You're going to dust them with aluminum powder. I've seen it done before. But I can save you the trouble, Detective Murphy. I can tell you ahead of time whose fingerprints they are. They belong to a gentleman named Ludwig Bull. He makes a business of breaking into people's houses. He's a lawyer and is probably collecting evidence. You see," Judy went on as the detective's eyes grew wider, "I work for a lawyer. We've solved several cases although we don't collect our evidence in quite this manner."

Dale turned to Judy.

"How did you know all this?" he demanded.

"The same way the detectives in your stories know things," she answered blandly, "by putting two and two together. The hole in this window is exactly like the hole that was broken in the window of my father's office at home. Ludwig Bull dropped his bankbook and it was as good as leaving a calling card behind him. Then Mrs. Merrit, Jane's mother, looked like a sheep-killing dog when I mentioned my father's name. That's where I went in the taxi, out to see Mrs. Merrit. The hospital gave me her address. And the lost bankbook was the mystery Irene was talking about. Well," Judy finished, "the story goes on from there. But the important thing is, we still haven't found Jane Merrit."

"What about Ludwig Bull?" Detective Murphy asked. "If what you say is true, we can nab him on a charge of breaking and entering. We may get a line on the girl from him."

"You're right," agreed Dale. "Are Judy and I invited? She has a bankbook to return and it may be a good ticket in case Mr. Bull hesitates about asking us in."

"Sure, come along." The detective waved his arms as though to include them both. "Why not? It's everybody's party."

"Speaking of parties," Judy said plaintively. "That reminds me, Dale, you were supposed to take me out to dinner."

"So help me," said the detective. "I forgot my dinner too. Let's phone the restaurant around the corner and have three dinners sent up. I'm beginning to like this place," he added, opening up the bridge table and placing it near the door.

"But what about Ludwig Bull?" Dale asked.

Detective Murphy shrugged his shoulders. "He can wait. We've done a good day's work already." And, calling from a telephone in an adjoining apartment, he ordered up three steaks with coffee and French fried potatoes. Judy could see that he didn't intend to let his work interfere with his pleasure.

"I should think," she said when he returned, "that if you find it so easy to borrow people's telephones you might ask our neighbors on the other side to turn off that phonograph."

"What's the use? I'm beginning to like that too," the detective said.

The phonograph provided still more atmosphere while they ate. It played nursery rhymes, popular songs, the *Humoresque*. And someone had just put on *The End of a Perfect Day* when Detective Murphy pushed back his plate and announced that they might as well be on their way.

But, at the door, Judy was seized with an impish impulse. The wax lady still stood by the window, her hand outstretched as if to bid them goodbye.

"Detective Murphy," begged Judy, "will you do me just one favor? You'll admit, I've helped you a little. But do you know who really invited us into this apartment? The wax lady. So won't you, just to please me, shake hands with her before we go?"

"Shake hands with her? Do you think I'm crazy?"

"No. Just grateful. Go ahead. Shake her

hand and thank her for the good time we've had. Please. I'd like to see you."

"Why, Miss Bolton, I'd be shot for a horse thief before I'd touch that wax woman's hand."

"I thought so." Judy smiled her satisfaction. "I just wanted to see how brave detectives really are. *I'm* not afraid to shake her hand."

"Let's get out of here," Detective Murphy muttered and, when they were on the elevator going down, Judy and Dale heard him say— almost to himself, "I'm not so sure that wax woman ain't alive after all."

CHAPTER XVII

LUDWIG BULL & SON

NINE o'clock that same evening found Dale's car parked before a pretentious stone dwelling in Brooklyn Heights. Detective Murphy was dozing at the wheel. The detective had decided it might be better for Judy and Dale to call on Mr. Bull by themselves. But they had agreed upon a shrill whistle which would signal the detective at once if he should be needed.

The Bull dwelling was situated on a corner with one side facing a business street and the other a quiet, residential street with other, equally pretentious stone houses built closely together. On the business street a small door opening directly to the sidewalk bore the legend LUDWIG BULL & SON, ATTORNEYS. But this entrance was quite dark.

On the other street was the entrance to the residential part of the house. This entrance was guarded by two stone lions. Judy was tempted to pat them as she and Dale ascended the curving steps to the lighted door.

A housemaid admitted them and Judy told

her they had come to return a bankbook that
Mr. Bull had lost.

"Mr. Bull is busy with a caller at the moment," the maid said, showing them in.
"Would you care to wait?"

They said they would and Dale immediately
found a magazine and began flipping its pages.
Judy looked about her, interested in the odd
room in which they found themselves. The
wall was papered with two kinds of paper and
a heavy rug of a peculiar yellow color covered
the floor. It was not, altogether, a restful
room. A stairway went upward from one side
while doors opened from the other three. One
of these was the entrance. The maid disappeared through another and so Judy guessed it
must lead to the servant's quarters. But a
light glimmered through a crack under the
third door and she could hear voices behind it.

Dale had seated himself beside the library
table near the entrance. But Judy, curious to
hear what was going on, tiptoed over and stood
beside the door to what she supposed must be
Ludwig Bull's library or, possibly, his office.
She could hear a woman's voice, high-pitched
and excited. She listened, quite sure she recog-
nized the voice.

"Our case is no good without the doctor's
testimony," it said, "and, under the circum-

stances I'm afraid it wouldn't be safe to fake it. Your friend might be faced by the real doctor —and then what? I can't afford to take the risk."

"I wouldn't worry about it if I were you, Mrs. Merrit——"

"Mrs. Merrit! I thought so," Judy whispered to herself. And this must be the voice of Ludwig Bull himself. He spoke more cautiously.

"The girl couldn't possibly have any knowledge of . . .

But now he had lowered his voice so that Judy could scarcely hear it.

Mrs. Merrit's voice, as she answered, was too faint for Judy to catch a word. But she thought plenty. It was her call to the Merrit estate that afternoon that had upset Mrs. Merrit and caused her to pay this hurried call. Undoubtedly, Ludwig Bull had been handling some sort of case in which she was interested. Judy was thankful for what little knowledge she had of the law. She strained her ears, but could not catch another word of the conversation that went on between Mrs. Merrit and her lawyer. Then she heard their footsteps as they approached the door and decided, suddenly, that she must find out what all this secrecy was about. As the door swung open, Judy darted behind it.

Ludwig Bull, still chattering with the buxom Mrs. Merrit, came out and escorted her to the front entrance. His back was turned now and Judy seized the opportunity, slipping around the corner and into the room he had just left. She was careful to close the door behind her. Ludwig Bull gave a little start, no doubt thinking it had closed by itself, and then turned to Dale.

"Well," he began pompously, "I hear you have found a bankbook with my name on it. The maid informed me. Would you mind telling me exactly when and where you found it?"

"I'd be glad to," Dale replied, "only I don't happen to be the one who found it. I merely came here with a friend of mine. She must have stepped outside."

"That's unfortunate. I always like to meet the ladies. Was she good enough to leave the bankbook with you?"

"Yes. I have it in my pocket."

And Dale produced the lost bankbook, meanwhile looking anxiously about the room. What had happened to Judy? She seemed to have vanished as completely as Jane.

"Is it yours?" he asked as the lawyer continued to study the bankbook.

"Not mine, but my son's. He is associated with me. I should very much like to know where he lost it."

"I'm sorry, but I can't tell you that."

"Well, it must have been somewhere in the city," Ludwig Bull reasoned. "Son!" he called to the room above. "Come down here and meet the gentleman who found your bankbook. He probably expects some reward."

Dale would have protested but just then a slick-haired youth of about twenty-five came noiselessly down the stairs.

"Thanks," he said, almost snatching the bankbook. "So you expect a reward, do you?"

"Only a little information," Dale said. "You might tell me what business you had in Farringdon last week."

"Say, what is this—a frame-up?" growled the youth. "I'm going out——"

Dale's shrill whistle sounded above his voice as he made for the front door.

"Thought you'd get away with it, didn't you?" Detective Murphy greeted him at the foot of the steps. "Well, you have a little explaining to do down at night court."

"Say, you can't do this. I'm Ludwig Bull——"

"So I gathered," chuckled the detective, slipping handcuffs over his wrists and leading him to the car. "You're arrested on charges of breaking and entering. It's just a little matter of checking up a few fingerprints."

"Detective Murphy," Dale asked in a lowered voice. "Did Judy come back to the car?"

"No, she didn't." He glanced about him. "Didn't she go into the Bull house with you?"

"Yes, and then I missed her."

At that moment the door to the darkened law office opened and Judy herself came running toward them with something white fluttering from her hand.

"What on earth?" exclaimed Dale as she collapsed, breathless, in the front seat beside him.

"I escaped just in time. He heard me," she panted, "and he came into the room with a gun in his hand. He looks fierce, doesn't he? Say, who's the prisoner?" she asked, turning to the detective in the seat behind her.

Dale had already started the car and they were speeding down Henry Street praying that the light would stay green.

"It's Ludwig Bull. Who did you suppose it would be?" Detective Murphy asked bluntly.

"But it was Ludwig Bull who had the gun," she protested. "He was chasing me."

"That's right," Dale told her. "There are two of them, father and son——"

"And both of them as crooked as they come," the detective added with a glance toward his squirming prisoner.

A police car passed and Detective Murphy hailed it.

"I think we can make better time, if you don't mind," he explained as he climbed out with his prisoner. "It was great to meet you, Mr. Meredith. I guess you got some ideas all right after tonight's performance. And thanks, Miss Bolton, for a pleasant evening."

"Is that dame's name Bolton?" the prisoner asked, glaring at Judy. "Then allow me to thank you, too, Miss Bolton, for a pleasant evening."

Judy blinked her eyes. "You know, Dale," she said, "I don't believe he likes me."

"Criminals usually don't. But tell me what happened to you. I'm not used to having young ladies vanish almost before my eyes."

"Well," she explained, "perhaps you didn't know it, but Ludwig Bull's lady caller was none other than Mrs. Merrit, Jane's mother-in-law. And she came there because of me. Apparently she was afraid I had found out something. Well, I haven't, but I mean to. I didn't want her to see me doing it so I slipped behind the door. Then Mr. Bull conveniently turned his back and I decided I might as well look through the papers he'd left on his desk."

"Well," Dale prompted her, "did you find anything?"

Her gray eyes glowed with triumph.

"I certainly did. Peter has taught me how to find things in a lawyer's office. I hadn't much time so I gathered things together as quickly as I could. You helped by keeping Mr. Bull busy outside. Naturally, I thought the detective had nabbed him when I heard your whistle. I didn't know about the son."

"And then what?"

"And then the door opened and there he stood. But I reached the outside door before he did and, with the police outside, he didn't dare fire his gun. I didn't think he would."

"Whew! That took courage. He could have fired. You often read of gangsters battling with the police."

"But not crooked lawyers," Judy said, contempt in her voice. "I hate them as much as Peter does. They're not brave, just sneaky, and I knew he wouldn't dare fire."

"But, Judy," Dale asked, "were these papers you found important enough for you to take that risk?"

"I think they were," she told him. And, as she spoke, she exhibited a manila folder. It was plainly marked EVIDENCE IN THE MERRIT CASE.

CHAPTER XVIII

JUDY awoke late the following morning and stretched herself luxuriously. Irene was standing in the doorway.

"Beulah has prepared a sumptuous breakfast," she announced. "Aren't you coming down and help us eat it?"

"Be down in a minute," Judy answered and began pulling on her stockings. It never took her very long to dress.

"Dale's down already," Irene went on. "He's like a different man. I thought it would do him good to get away from that story. But I can't make anything out of all this talk about detectives and police cars and stolen evidence. Did it really happen or did you and Dale see one of these mystery thrillers at the movies? I thought you were going to visit Jane."

"We did," Judy said. She was just pulling a dress over her head and her voice was somewhat muffled. "I mean we did visit the apartment but Jane wasn't there. We prowled around a bit and met a wax lady and almost got arrested and then went with a detective and ar-

rested someone else. And who do you think it
was?"

"I can't imagine. It all sounds like a fairy
tale to me. Are you sure you're quite awake?"
Irene asked anxiously.

"Quite. And also in my right senses. You
haven't any plans for the day, have you?"

"Well, not especially——"

"Then I have plans for you. We're going
through this evidence together."

Irene looked bewildered.

"What evidence? Do talk sensibly, Judy.
First you're arresting somebody and now you
have evidence. I thought the evidence came
first."

"It usually does," Judy said, giving a last
pat to her hair. "Well, I'm ready for breakfast. The evidence will keep."

All during the meal Dale and Judy chattered
over the events of the evening before until, at
last, Irene began to have a vague picture in her
mind of what had happened. She was thankful, she said, that she wasn't there. It sounded
altogether too exciting for her quiet tastes.

"But what did you do with your evening?"
Dale asked her.

"Nothing much. Sylvia and I chattered and
I showed off the baby. She's such a lamb. I
love her more every minute. It's much nicer
being at home with your very own precious

baby than running about in empty apartments solving mysteries. Dale, I'm surprised that you don't pay more attention to Judy Irene. You did at first."

Dale gave a guilty start. "Did I? Well, what is a man to do with a little mite of a baby? I thought you were going to hire a nursemaid."

"I've just about decided not to," Irene told him. "Judy Irene is more important than singing on the radio and I'm sure I could never find a nursemaid to suit me. I'd be jealous of her. Really, Dale, I love that child so much that I could never turn her over to a perfect stranger. I wish Judy could just stay here with me and then we could look after her together."

"But that's impossible—" Judy began, her heart in her mouth for fear of what else Irene might say.

"I know it," she sighed. "I'm always wanting the impossible. But this house is so big and it seems so empty sometimes. It isn't as though any of the neighbors came in to visit. I don't even know them. I do get lonely."

"Blame me," Dale said. "It's this beastly writing."

"But it's your work," Irene protested. "I want you to do it. Don't think I want to take you away from your work."

"Well then, if you'll excuse me, I'll get back to it," he answered abruptly and, pushing his chair away from the table, he started upstairs to his writing room.

Judy and Irene looked at each other. Irene's expression was a puzzled one, but Judy's was eager. The whole day lay ahead of her and upstairs, on her dresser, was the manila envelope marked EVIDENCE IN THE MERRIT CASE.

"I'll get those papers about Jane Merrit and we can go over them while Judy Irene is having her nap," she suggested.

"She has to have her bath first."

"All right. But after that."

Irene wasn't as interested as Judy thought she would be. But then, she had no idea that finding Jane was really just the same as finding her own baby. Judy watched her as she lifted the little pink form out of the bathtub and couldn't help wondering how Irene would ever stand the shock of hearing that this baby —the baby that she loved—was really Jane's. But never to tell her? That would be even worse. Dale might escape into a story or into an adventure like the one of the previous night. But the fact that Irene was bringing up the wrong baby would stand like a ghost between them for the rest of his life.

The baby, pink as a rosebud after her bath, was now tucked into her carriage. Irene kissed the little hand and then turned to Judy.

"All right, dear. Get your evidence if you

want to.   Maybe I can forget Judy Irene long
enough to think about it.   If it concerns Jane,
as you say, I really should be interested for I
was very fond of her.   But I feel, somehow,
that she's safe when she's missing.   If her in-
laws don't know where she is they can't be making her unhappy, can they?   And I'm not at all
sure it's wise to try and find her."

"Do you think she'll ever get in touch with
you, Irene?" asked Judy.

She thought about it a minute, then answered
slowly, "I really don't think so.   My telephone
number was in that pocketbook her husband
took and she doesn't have my address.   She
might look it up in the phone book but there
are at least a half a dozen Merediths and she
wouldn't bother unless it was important.   Often you meet people like that, make friends
and then never see them again.   Ships that pass
in the night——"

"Oh, stop!" Judy begged.   "You make it
all sound so sad.   Of course you'll see Jane
again."

"Unless it was important," Judy thought.
Jane would consider it important if she noticed
the bracelet with *MEREDITH* on it instead of
MERRIT.   But the names were so much alike
she might not notice it for days.   Besides, she
might have removed the bracelet from the
baby's arm and put it away without looking at

it. But some day, when she did look, she'd see the wrong name.

Judy decided that, if the telephone rang, either she or Dale ought to answer it.

In the meantime she and Irene would find out as much about Jane as they could from the papers inside the manila folder. They settled themselves on the sofa with the papers and a box of candy between them. Then Judy, her heart beating a little faster, opened the folder. The first thing that fell out was a letter; then a bunch of torn pages from someone's diary.

"That's Jane's handwriting," Irene declared. "It must be hers. Let's see what's in it."

Lady Isabel may help me out of this mess I'm in, they read. *I bought her today at an auction and we rode home together in a taxi. I guess we scared a few people. Lady Isabel is quite ghostly but I can touch her up with a little rouge. She was practically naked and I felt so ashamed for her but, once we were home, I dolled her all up in my graduation dress. I talk to her as though she were a friend. To tell you the truth, dear diary, she is about the only friend I have . . .*

Irene put down the page. She was really interested now.

"Who is this Lady Isabel?" she asked.

"I think I can tell you that. Remember the

wax lady I told you about at breakfast?
Well," Judy said, "it isn't so odd that Jane
should have named her Lady Isabel. I thought
of naming her Lady Elizabeth myself."

"But what sort of evidence is this?" Irene
questioned. "All these things are marked 'evidence.' "

"We'll see," Judy promised, "when we read
a little further."

But, as they read more letters and papers,
the whole thing became more puzzling. There
was no evidence of anything except that Jane
had been lonely and had liked to imagine that
trees and birds—in fact everything that
pleased her—could talk with her and understand her thoughts. The letter on top of the
pile was one she had written to herself.

Dear Jane, she had written. *I think I ought
to tell you in black and white just what I think
of you for believing any of the lies HE told you.
You should have had better sense. If you had
had the right sort of upbringing you would
have known from the first that he merely
wanted another puppet for his mother to push
around. SHE DRIVES ME WILD. She
drives both of us wild. I sometimes look at you
in the mirror and you look just as wild as I do.
It's funny, isn't it? I ought to call you Insane
Jane, you silly girl in the mirror.*

"That girl can write. What imagination!"

Irene exclaimed. "I'll have to show this to Dale. He says the best practice in the world for a professional writer is to write down his thoughts just the way they come into his head. And that's exactly what Jane was doing. She always spoke of her husband as HE. You could almost hear her capitalize it. Really, it must be terrible to be married to a man you don't love. And that mother-in-law! I wonder what she said when *she* read what Jane thought of her."

"Maybe she's suing Jane for slander or something," Judy suggested.

"I don't think so," Irene protested. "How could she, when Jane hasn't any money?"

"Did she ever say anything to you about how she meant to support herself and the baby, Irene?"

"Yes, plenty of times," Irene answered. "She had all kinds of ideas. She mentioned the dress shop, for one thing. She also mentioned writing. That was when I told her Dale was a writer. She said she wrote too, but only nonsense in order to get her mind off her troubles. Well, we've seen a sample of that. Now I'd like to see her try a real story."

"I would too," Judy agreed. "She's had experience enough, poor girl! But what else did she mention?"

"She said she'd be willing to do anything but

she'd never let her husband's mother take the baby away——"

"So that was what the old dragon wanted to do?" Judy interrupted. "I might have known it. Do you know, Irene, all this evidence may have something to do with getting possession of the baby."

"But that's just it," laughed Irene. "She can't when she doesn't know where the baby is. That's why I don't understand your attitude at all, Judy. Jane doesn't want to be found. Or is it just because you're curious and like to solve mysteries? Dale said you were having an awfully good time last night."

"I was," Judy admitted. "I guess I'm just a natural born snoop. But let's go on snooping. What's this?" And Judy held up a white card with a great many things written on it in a hand that looked—yes, that *was* familiar. She jumped to her feet, dropping the rest of the evidence in a heap on the floor.

"Well, I have solved a mystery!" she cried, waving the card. "And here's the case history that goes with it. I knew Ludwig Bull wanted more than a piece of pie when he sneaked into our house through the window. Irene, your friend Jane Merrit was my father's patient several years ago. I don't understand these medical terms but I soon will. I'm going to call Dad on the telephone!"

CHAPTER XIX

LONG DISTANCE, PLEASE!

"Long distance," Judy told the operator excitedly over the telephone. "Yes, I want to talk with Dr. H. H. Bolton. The number is Farringdon six thousand. Yes, I'll wait."

The wire buzzed faintly for a minute and then Judy heard her father's voice as clearly as though he had been right in the room.

"Hello, Dad? Oh, Dad! This is Judy. I guess you know it. Dad, I've found out why that man broke into your office window. He wanted to get hold of some of your records. You had a patient, Jane Merrit—no, her name was Jane Dwyer then. And this thief took both her card and the case history so you couldn't check one with the other. Yes, we know who he was. Ludwig Bull, a crook lawyer. We traced him through that bankbook he lost. Yes. Yes, he wanted evidence. Horace can have that much for his paper. I'm sure he'll love me for it. There are two Ludwig Bulls, tell him, both crooks and both working together. It was the younger one who broke into our house. But, Dad, what could he have learned from your medical records?"

"Jane Dwyer. Let me see." The doctor's voice sounded perplexed over the wire. "Oh, yes. She was that little millworker. She had been working too hard and came to me with some nervous disorder. I don't remember exactly what it was."

"It says *neurasthenia* on the card."

"That's just a general term for a run-down condition and sick nerves. It was brought on by overwork and unhappy conditions at home. She lived with an exacting relative here in Farringdon and I advised her to leave home. In fact, I think I recommended a certain girls' club in New York. A change of scene is often better than a tonic for such an ailment. But the girl was only sixteen. I can't imagine why anyone should think it necessary to steal her medical records. They weren't important and I predicted a complete recovery. But tell me about yourself now, Judy girl. Are you all right?"

"Yes. I'm all right." Judy hesitated. There were so many things she longed to tell her father.

"Was the baby as wonderful as you thought she would be? And how is the little mother?"

"She's all right. I mean, they're all right. Isn't this costing a lot of money, Dad? I spent nearly all I had on a taxicab. It took me way out on Long Island."

"Reverse the charges. Why didn't you tell me you needed money? I'll mail a check at once. Is that all that's worrying you?"

"That's about all."

"Now come on, tell your old Dad," he urged. "What about this taxicab ride out on Long Island? I can tell from the sound of your voice that you're in a peck of trouble."

"It's mostly about Jane. This girl who was your patient. She's missing, Dad. And her husband's people are trying to trump up some charge against her so they can take her baby away from her when they find her. Dad, I wish I could talk with Peter about it. There's something else too. Will you tell Peter—but never mind," she broke off. "I'll tell him my-self when I get home. Is Mother there? Let me just say hello to her before I hang up."

Judy's hello to her mother sounded cheerful enough and she was able to close the conversation without saying anything that she thought would worry her. She turned from the tele-phone to see Irene standing beside her with a dictionary in her hand.

"I heard that word you used and looked it up. See what it says, *neurasthenia, derange-ment of the nervous system*. And then I looked up *derangement* and it says, *unbalanced rea-son, insanity!* So you see what this evidence is. They're trying to prove that Jane is insane so they can take her baby away. That's what Mrs. Merrit was seeing the lawyer about and she's probably offered him enough money so that he feels he can afford to break a few laws to get his evidence. And if you and Dale keep on looking for Jane you'll just be helping them and I won't forgive either of you—ever! It's a contemptible thing to do. Jane's no more insane than you and I are. She only called herself Insane Jane for a joke and you said yourself you thought of naming the wax woman Lady Elizabeth. But they're going to try and prove this about Jane because she named the wax woman Lady Isabel and because she wrote a letter to herself. Oh, Judy!" Irene finished, almost hysterical now. "Can't you see what you'll be doing if you help them find her?"

Judy let the paper flutter from her hand. Yes, she could see. She had been in the court-room often enough to see how clever lawyers win their cases through the vilest trickery. She had seen Peter lose such a case. Yes, the Vincent case was like that and if it hadn't been for her midnight visitor . . .

But that was past now. It was solved and done with. This wasn't. Would it ever be, Judy wondered. Puzzle as she would, she could see no way out of it. Detective Murphy was working for the police and they were helping Mrs. Merrit—not Jane. And Jane had the wrong baby. By now Judy was sure she couldn't know it. But it meant that little Judy Irene—Judy's namesake, Dale's and Irene's very own baby—would be brought up by that awful Mrs. Jiggs-Jordan-Merrit. That dragon! It was too terrible to contemplate.

"I wish Peter were here," Judy said at last. "He'd know what to do. He always does."

"But then," Irene reminded her, "you'd have to tell him about the diamond you lost out of your ring."

"Well," Judy retorted thoughtlessly, "I want to tell him everything. I'm sick of keeping secrets——"

A shadow fell across the floor and Dale appeared in the doorway. He was scowling darkly.

"Go to your room," he commanded as though Judy were a child. "I can't have you upsetting Irene in this manner. If you can't control yourself any better than this——"

"But, Dale, it was my fault," Irene defended her. "I was storming at her too. Sit down and let me tell you about it."

Judy, upstairs, knew that she must not give way to tears again. But her throat ached from trying to choke them back. It was all so tragic. If Jane remained missing she and Irene might both be happy with each other's babies—not knowing. But some day it would come out that she, Judy, had kept the secret. Dale would go about with a haunted look on his face and soon the happiness Irene had thought she had found just wouldn't exist any more. There wasn't a chance of their ever being happy again with such a secret between them.

Last night, Judy remembered, she had actually enjoyed herself. It seemed impossible now. And yet, when she was solving a mystery she could forget everything else and enjoy the adventure for adventure's sake. That was what she had done. But now there wouldn't be any adventure. She couldn't help Detective Murphy. She couldn't help Dale and Irene.

"All I've done is hurt people," she told herself miserably. And the whole thing seemed to be her fault. She had gone with Dale and helped him select those twin baby clothes and she had lost her diamond. Those were the reasons, and the only reasons, for the babies being mixed up.

"I did it and I ought to undo it. But how can I?" she asked herself over and over.

The day dragged on. Judy found things to keep her hands busy, helping Irene. But nothing could keep her from thinking. Even when something cheered her for a moment she would look at her hand, see the empty setting and be reminded that everything was wrong.

"If only I could talk it over with someone—with Peter," thought Judy. She had never realized how much she needed him before. There was no one in the world as dependable as Peter.

"I can write to him anyway," she decided the following morning and as soon as she and Irene had the baby bathed and ready for her nap she sat down at the desk in the living room.

Dear Peter, she began. *I miss you terribly. What wouldn't I give to be back at the office with everything straightened out here so that I could leave. It all began to be wrong at the hospital when a man brushed past me on the stairs and knocked the diamond out of my ring. Peter, I couldn't find it. I'm heartbroken about it and hardly know how to tell you. And then, while we were searching——*

"No, I can't tell him that," she said to herself and ripped the paper into tiny shreds.

Dear Peter, she began again. *Here I am at Tower House with Dale and Irene. We have been so busy that I haven't had time to write before. Dale is helping me solve a mystery——*

"But he isn't," she thought. Besides, she couldn't tell Peter that. He was the one who always helped her solve her mysteries.

This time she tore the paper into ribbons and crumpled them all together. It was funny about Peter. You couldn't tell him anything but the truth. Perhaps that was why she loved him.

An hour later she was still starting letters to Peter and tearing them up when a familiar footstep outside on the porch interrupted her. Could it be? Yes, it *was* Peter. She flew to the door and almost flung herself into his arms.

"Peter! Peter!" she cried, half laughing and half sobbing, "I do have a fairy godmother who grants wishes. Just when I was thinking I couldn't live another minute without you, here you are!"

"Were you honestly thinking that?" he asked, tilting her chin so that he could see straight into her eyes.

"Yes, I was." She pulled him inside. "If you don't believe it, just look at that waste-paper basket. It's filled with things I was trying to say to you and couldn't—because you weren't here."

"Well, say them now, Angel." He handed her his clean handkerchief. "And, for Heaven's sake, dry your eyes. You don't look well in tears."

She took the handkerchief in her left hand. But, as she raised it to dry her eyes, she saw the look that crossed Peter's face. He had seen the empty setting! He knew! Now she wouldn't need to tell him.

CHAPTER XX

PETER'S PLAN

"WHERE did you lose it, Angel?" Peter asked gently. "Tell me all about it. Maybe we can still find it but, even if we can't, how many times do I have to tell you that it isn't the ring that matters. It's what it stands for."

"I know that, Peter. I know it so much better than I did before. I've learned how much I need you, if nothing else—and how much I love you. I'm not sure of anything else, but I am sure of that. I had to wear the ring even without the diamond because I cared so much I couldn't take it off."

"So that's what it was——"

"But that wasn't all," she interrupted. "There was something else I wanted to tell you."

"I suspected as much. I came because your father was worried after he talked with you on the telephone. I thought perhaps you were homesick. I drove in and you can ride back with me if you are."

"But, Peter, I can't go back," Judy protested. "I must find Jane first. No, I mustn't

161

find Jane. Irene says I mustn't but if I don't—
Oh, Peter! I *wish* I could tell you.''

"Go right ahead and tell me," he urged.
"I'm listening. Who is Jane? Your father
mentioned a Jane Dwyer whose medical history was stolen. Is she the one?''

"She's Jane Merrit now. Irene met her at
the hospital when they had their babies. And
now she's missing and her in-laws are going to
take the baby away from her if they find her.
That's why I can't help. And Peter, there's
something more that I can't tell you because I
promised. But there's a reason why I must
find her. It's going to make someone terribly
unhappy unless I do.''

"Then, of course, you must," Peter agreed.
"But about this baby business. I hardly see
how anyone could take a baby away from its
own mother if she is able to take care of it herself. What about her husband? Doesn't he
have anything to say?''

"He says whatever his mother wants him to
—and she's terrible. I met her," Judy said.
"She's rich—awfully rich. She thinks money
buys everything, even her son's baby, and she's
paid this lawyer wads of money, I'm sure.
They're going to try and prove that Jane is
insane. I know it. And she isn't any more
than I am. She's one of the sweetest, most lovable girls I ever met.''

"It looks as though she might need a lawyer then," Peter commented. "Her in-laws probably intend to bring suit for the custody of the child but any judge with two eyes in his head and a heart in his body would think twice before taking a new-born baby away from its mother."

"It sounds simple the way you say it. But what are we going to do if we can't find Jane?"

"We'll find her all right, if it's that important to you," Peter promised. "We found Irene when she was lost, didn't we? And we found Lorraine that time she and her fur coat both disappeared right after the fur shop was robbed. I'd say you and I have done very well without the aid of the Missing Persons Bureau. And now, Judy girl, if you'll tell me everything you can about Jane Merrit, I'll try and work out some sort of a plan."

Judy tried to tell him as much as she could but she kept hesitating for fear of telling about the babies. At last she thought of something that would explain things better than she could.

"I'll show you the evidence," she offered. "I got it from Mrs. Merrit's lawyer. Just wait!"

And in a minute Judy returned with the manila folder. Peter's eyes opened in surprise.

"What sort of a lawyer is he, to give you

this? He can't think very much of his case or he'd never let it out of his hands."

"He didn't," Judy confessed. "I stole it when Dale and I went to return his bankbook. I think somebody said once, 'It's no crime to steal from a thief.' And he got this evidence by breaking into my father's office and Jane's apartment. He's one of these crook lawyers, the kind that always make your cases so difficult."

Peter studied the contents of the manila envelope for fully ten minutes before he answered. Then he said, "Without this evidence, I don't see how anyone could prove that Jane Merrit is not legally sane. Surely, no doctor would testify against her and, without a doctor's testimony, her mother-in-law wouldn't stand a chance of winning the case."

"But, Peter, I heard her lawyer say something about faking a doctor's testimony. He might even bribe a friend to pose as my father——"

Peter chuckled. "That would show him up. I'd just like to see him try it with you in the courtroom."

"Then you think Jane's mother-in-law really hasn't any case at all?"

"I'm practically sure of it. But there is one thing, if Jane has to depend on her husband for support she may be obliged to go back to him.

She can't get a divorce in New York state and she can't leave without money. I don't see how she's managed this long unless some friend is helping her.''

"But she hasn't a friend. We know that from her diary.''

"Then perhaps some kindhearted landlady has rented her a room and offered to mind her baby while she looks for work. She may be tramping the streets this minute or sitting on a park bench searching through the HELP WANTED ads. Say!'' Peter said suddenly. "Couldn't we put an ad in the paper and find her?''

"I knew you'd think of something,'' Judy declared. "That's the very thing. Irene wants a nursemaid and we'll advertise for one. I'm sure she'll agree to it if I tell her I'm going home with you. She does want to keep up her radio work, in spite of what she says, and she can't unless we find a nursemaid.''

"Of course,'' Peter mused, "there's only a slim chance of finding Jane through an ad. We'll try and think up a suitable one this afternoon if Irene agrees to it. In the meantime, Judy, I'm beginning to wonder. Doesn't anybody live in this house except you? We've been sitting here talking for more than an hour and I haven't seen a trace of Dale or Irene or the baby. Where do they keep themselves?''

"Dale's in his writing room. He's worse than a hermit. The baby is asleep in the nursery and I'll soon find out where Irene is. Irene!" Judy called.

The golden-haired girl appeared almost immediately.

"Well, it's about time you let us know you were here, Peter Dobbs," she scolded. "I peeked in and saw you sitting there with Judy and thought I'd leave you alone until she had explained things."

"She has. Quite fully. How well you're looking, Irene," Peter commented. "Motherhood must agree with you. Now may I see the prodigy?"

"You go up to the nursery with him," Judy urged, "while I go out and tell Beulah to hurry up lunch. I know he's starved and I thought maybe, if I made an apple pie, it might seem a little more like a welcome."

Peter threw her a grateful look over his shoulder as he followed Irene up the stairs. Next to blackberry tarts, apple pie was his favorite dessert. But Judy was not really interested in the pie. She knew she couldn't look at Peter over that baby's crib without letting her eyes give away the secret.

CHAPTER XXI

HELP WANTED—FEMALE

DALE came down to lunch when Beulah announced, "Dere's company, sah! An' Miss Judy's done baked a pie."

She was rather a heavy colored girl but she always tiptoed when she came near Dale's study, half in awe of the "gencmen who writes." Dale's moods, these last few days, were enough to fill anyone with awe. His greeting was a little cold, Judy thought, and lunch was quiet and strained until she brought in the pie.

Judy was no artist. She knew that. But pie crusts were such a temptation that she always tried to cut out a picture of something with a knife.

"What is it? The Toonerville Trolley?" asked Peter, viewing the sketch.

"Is it that bad? I tried to make a picture of your car," confessed Judy. "I'll be riding in it soon. Irene, did Peter tell you he is taking me home in his car?"

"How soon is he leaving?" Dale asked almost as if he would be glad to see him go.

167

"Well, not until I do," Judy said, "and I'm staying until Irene finds a nursemaid."

"I thought I told you I'd decided to do without one," Irene told her. "It's fun looking after Judy Irene and I don't see why I need to hire a woman to do it when I can just as well look after her myself."

"You'll be tied down every single evening," Judy reminded her. "You know how Beulah has to hurry home to her own family as soon as the dinner dishes are done at night. And you'll have to give up your radio work and everything. Now I think, instead of bothering with employment agencies, it would be a good idea to put ads in the papers and have the girls come out here to be interviewed. I'll make up an ad that will be sure to appeal to the right type of girl. Will you let me do it, Irene?"

"Oh, I don't care. Of course I'd be glad to have a nursemaid for Judy Irene if you could find a girl I really liked. She'd be company for me."

"We'll advertise for a nursemaid and companion then. What do you think of it, Dale?" Judy asked.

"I think it ought to have been done three days ago, before Irene got so attached to the youngster," he answered unexpectedly.

"He's jealous," giggled Irene. "I've heard

of husbands being jealous of their own babies but I never thought Dale would be like that. He hardly looks at the poor lamb. Somebody has to be nice to her."

"Let the nursemaid be nice to her then. It's time you had one."

Irene turned toward Peter and Judy and shrugged her shoulders. It was the best apology she could offer for Dale's bearish behavior. Judy could see she was hurt and felt very sorry for her. But she felt even sorrier for Dale.

After the meal Peter drew Judy aside and said, "I see what you're afraid of, Judy, even if I don't quite understand it. Dale has changed terribly. He's in some trouble, isn't he?"

Judy nodded but said nothing.

"And he's asked you to keep it secret, hasn't he?"

"Yes," Judy admitted. "I was angry at first but now I don't know what else I can do. Finding Jane may help and it may only make matters worse. I don't expect you to understand it, Peter. But you'll trust me, won't you?"

"I always do, Judy."

"Then let's compose that ad and get it in the papers as quickly as possible. I want it in all the papers so that, if Jane's looking for work, she can't miss it. And we must word it so that it sounds as attractive as possible."

"How would this be? NURSEMAID, refined Christian girl——"

"No, I don't like that. I don't like mentioning religion. Maybe Jane isn't Christian. I never asked her."

"Well, then, INTELLIGENT YOUNG WOMAN as nursemaid and companion——"

"No, that won't do either," Judy declared. "Any one of a hundred girls might fit that description and I want an ad that will appeal only to Jane. We really haven't time to interview swarms of young women."

Peter agreed. But what could they say that would appeal only to Jane? Judy seated herself at the writing desk, took a pencil in her hand and began to concentrate.

"I have it!" she exclaimed at last. And she began writing quickly:

YOUNG WOMAN WITH BABY, intelligent, refined, as companion and nursemaid in home with only child.   PARKVILLE 6–7675

"A stroke of genius," Peter commented when he read it.

"It may be," Judy agreed modestly, "but Irene won't like it. We'll have to insert it without her knowing it. Then you and I will have a secret to even things up.''

"I'd better telephone it in from the drug-store.''

"And don't forget a single paper,'' Judy cautioned him. "YOUNG WOMAN WITH BABY goes in caps. And have them insert it twice in each paper, once under household help and once in the regular help wanted section.''

"What about the Personals?''

"That might look suspicious, as though we were setting a trap for someone. I wish I could be perfectly sure we aren't.''

"We don't have to feed the mouse to the cat even if we do catch it,'' Peter said. "The cat hasn't a chance.''

"Meaning Mrs. Jiggs-Jordan-Merrit, of course. I think I'll rename her 'cunning old Fury.' You remember the Mouse's Tale?''

"She can't be judge and jury in American courts,'' laughed Peter. "This isn't Wonder-land.''

"I'll think it is,'' Judy declared, "if this scheme works and everything comes out all right. It's such a mess now. Remember, Pe-ter, the ad is to run indefinitely.''

"I'll remember. I'll put it in just as you've written it,'' Peter promised, "capital letters and all.''

Judy watched him as he hurried off with the paper in his pocket.

"Dear Peter," she murmured. "Dear, dependable Peter. I wouldn't change a hair on his head. No, not even the pug in his nose. And only a little while ago I was wondering how I could be sure I loved him."

Irene came in a little later and found Judy still dreaming at the window.

"I thought you were going to call up the papers and put in an advertisement for a nursemaid," she said.

Judy gave a little start.

"Oh, that's done already," she replied.

"Done!" Irene exclaimed. "And you didn't tell me? I should think I ought to have something to say about the kind of a girl I want. How was it worded?"

"Something about a nursemaid and companion, refined, intelligent and all that. I can't tell you exactly. Peter helped me compose it."

"And what paper was it in? I wanted it to be in the *Post* because I think intelligent people are apt to see it there."

"It was," Judy said. She didn't add that it was in all the other papers as well.

"Where's Peter now? I thought we might have a game together to pass the time, or did you have other things to do?"

"Not another thing," Judy said. It was

true. Now that the ad was in, she hadn't a thing to do except wait for the telephone to ring. "Peter went out to the drugstore for a minute but he'll be right back," she added.

Peter took longer than Judy thought he would and when he did return he had a large box of candy under his arm. He had also purchased a gift for Irene's baby.

"Open it," he directed, handing her a very tiny package.

"I know what it is already!" she exclaimed delightedly. "A little spoon. Peter, how dear of you to think of a spoon. Everyone else has given her clothes but this is a reminder that she will be a big girl—and feed herself."

She unwrapped the spoon and looked at it more closely. The baby's name was engraved on the handle—*Judy Irene.*

"And she's really Jane," thought Judy, turning her face away. "Even Peter doesn't know it. But Dale does—and he's going to hate that spoon with the wrong name——"

"I think I'll go up and show it to Dale," Irene announced. "He wasn't very nice to Peter this noon and he'll be sorry when he sees the nice present he brought——"

"Wait a minute!" Judy pulled Irene back to the sofa. "Weren't we going to have a game? I'm sure Dale wouldn't want to be bothered seeing a present now. His typewriter was going like mad this morning and I'm sure he's still busy——"

"Well, he shouldn't be!" Irene exploded, tears suddenly filling her blue eyes. "I've stood this just about as long as I intend to, Judy. You and Dale both act just as if I shouldn't have had a baby. Everything was all right before you came and now everything's all wrong. Even the baby isn't as well as she was. Listen, I hear her crying now."

"I'll go up to her," Judy offered, glad of an excuse to get away.

She lifted the wailing baby out of her crib and began patting her back. The formula that the doctor had prepared for the real Judy Irene was a little too strong for this baby and seemed to be giving it colic. Judy knew that much from reading her father's medical books. She still had the baby over her shoulder when she returned to the living room.

"It's colic," she announced. "The food isn't right or something. You could make it a little weaker."

"I don't intend to experiment with the baby's food," Irene declared positively. "If she isn't better by tomorrow I'll take her to a doctor."

"A doctor!" gasped Judy, alarmed at the thought. "Not the same doctor you had in the hospital?"

"I don't see why not.   He's a good man."

"But—but—" Judy stammered helplessly. She couldn't cry out, as she wanted to, "But the doctor will know. The doctor will know this is Jane's baby, not yours. They'll know it at the hospital too. They have the baby's footprints."

At that moment Dale appeared at the door. The baby's crying had interrupted his writing for the day. Judy's eyes sought his, pleading for a way out.

"What's the trouble?" he wanted to know. "What's the baby yelling about?"

"Judy says it's colic," Peter explained. "Irene is taking her to the doctor——"

"She's doing no such thing," Dale interrupted. "If the baby has to see a doctor I'll take her myself—not to that crank of a doctor we had. But to a child specialist."

Irene stared at him. So did Peter. But Judy understood the reason and said thankfully, "You see, Irene, Dale does care a great deal about the baby. An ordinary doctor won't do for his daughter. She has to have the best there is."

"And the best nursemaid," Peter added, beginning to see light.

Irene carried the baby back to the nursery after telling Dale it was a funny way of caring. Dale stalked out of the house and Peter, left alone with Judy, said in a low voice, "I'd like to know this much. What did those babies wear in the hospital? Were there tapes on their wrists to identify them or did thy wear bracelets——"

Judy interrupted wildly. "If you mention that word to me, I'll scream. I swear it. I'll scream and faint. And I haven't told you a thing, Peter Dobbs, not a solitary thing."

"All right," Peter said. "You haven't. But just the same, I begin to understand the importance of finding Jane."

CHAPTER XXII

WHILE THEY WAITED

JUDY had never before thought of a telephone as much more than an instrument of communication. It summoned help in time of need and brought her in touch with friends when she was lonely. It was not until after she and Peter knew their ad was actually in all the morning papers that it became a living thing with a voice that might be Jane's.

Once Judy had seen some sketches in a pictorial magazine that were supposed to illustrate how a fly sees everything in little cubes and how a hen sees the thing on which her eye is focused much larger than anything else. For instance, a hen sees a rooster towering above all the other creatures in the farmyard. Thus Judy saw the telephone. It was a giant now, towering above every other thing in Tower House. Whenever it rang Judy dived for it as madly as though a fire alarm had sounded. And each time she turned away, disappointed, to summon Irene or Dale. The morning dragged on and still not a single person called in answer to the YOUNG WOMAN WITH BABY ad.

"I should be the one to look worried," Irene

remarked as Judy stood disconsolately beside the telephone table. "How do I know the ad got into the papers at all?"

"Because Peter put it in," Judy answered with implicit trust.

"Well, I'll have to see it myself before I'll believe it," she declared. "There aren't so many positions available that not a single person would call in answer to an advertisement for a nursemaid."

Peter and Judy exchanged glances. Suppose Irene looked for the ad and saw how they had worded it! She would be angry, they both knew. They had purposely mislaid the morning *Times* after Dale had glanced at the headlines over his coffee. Later Irene dozed on the sofa, finishing her night's sleep. The baby had kept everyone awake screaming with colic. Now she was sleeping peacefully and Judy knew why. She had prepared her formula that morning and made it just as weak as she dared. But after her next bottle, prepared by Irene, she began screaming and drawing up her legs in pain. Dale strode into the nursery at eleven o'clock declaring he could stand it no longer.

"Get her into her bunting and we'll take her to a specialist," he said. "I'll go for the car."

"I'm coming with you," Irene announced. "You'll forget half the things the doctor tells you."

"The specialist!" he almost snapped.

"Oh, all right, the specialist. But I'm going anyway. Where is this miracle man you want her to see?"

Dale picked up the Brooklyn Red Book and selected a child specialist at random. It was a downtown address. Joralemon Street.

"He probably won't be any better than our own doctor. He'll only charge more," Irene said peevishly as they started off.

Judy and Peter, at the window, watched them out of sight.

"What a tragedy for both of them!" said Peter.

"It is, isn't it?" agreed Judy realizing that he knew, even though she had not told him.

The house seemed strangely quiet after they had gone. Only the heavy footsteps of Beulah upstairs dusting and making beds sounded through the silence. Why didn't the telephone ring? Now, with Dale and Irene gone, Judy could talk freely to Jane without being overheard. But she was beginning to think Jane would never call.

"Cheer up," Peter told her, tilting her chin and looking into her troubled gray eyes. "The evening papers are out at noon."

"It's noon now."

"I suppose we ought to eat then. Do I hear Beulah in the kitchen or shall we fix something ourselves?"

The voice of Beulah herself answered them.

"Lunch is ready, Miss Judy. It's so quiet with dat baby gone I done scare myself if I call. Lordy, how loud dat phone rings!"

"I'll take it, Beulah."

"An answer to the ad?" Peter questioned when Judy joined him a little later at the table.

"A man selling vacuum cleaners," she answered in disgust. "I told him we didn't clean our floors."

Peter chuckled and dipped into his soup. But neither of them finished what Beulah had served them.

"Do you know, it's rather restful to have the baby out of the house," Judy said as they walked back into the living room. "I keep looking at it and feeling so sorry for it. What kind of a future does it have, the poor thing, with Dale knowing? He'll never love it as he would his own and Irene will love it all the more fiercely in defense. Sometimes I think there's a jinx on Tower House and nobody ever can be happy in it. None of Irene's relatives ever have been."

"Don't let me hear you voicing that opinion when Irene's around," Peter chided her.

"I wont. You know that. Anyway, I'm not superstitious. But it's true, a house does borrow the personalities of the people who live in it. You should have seen that Merrit place out on Long Island. For all it was so rich and splendid, it was really rather frightening because Mrs. Jiggs-Jordan-Merrit's personality spoiled everything beautiful about it. A house is either a pleasant place or an unpleasant one, depending on what the people make it."

"But look at your house," Peter pointed out. "There's none of old Vine Thompson's personality left in it now that you are living there."

"I think there is," Judy said. "Anyway, enough to make it interesting. Think of all the mysteries we've solved because of her."

"They seem easy, now that we're up against one that we can't solve. If this ad brings no results, I confess, we're up against a brick wall. Jane doesn't want to be found, that's clear, and if she doesn't want a job——"

"But, Peter," Judy interrupted. "She has to live. She hasn't any money or any friends and I don't see how she could leave New York without money."

"It's been done."

"You mean hitchhiking and things? But that's dangerous for a girl alone, and think of the baby! I can't believe she would——"

But Judy did not finish her sentence. The telephone was ringing again and she darted for it.

"Hello!" Her voice became excited. "Yes, we advertised. You have a child two years old? No, I'm afraid not. We wanted a nursemaid with a very young baby. I know it's unusual. I'm sorry. Perhaps you'll find a position somewhere else."

Judy sighed and turned away from the telephone.

"It wasn't Jane," she said unnecessarily.

The next time the telephone rang it was Irene calling to say that she and Dale would not be home for lunch.

"I suppose you've finished anyway," she added.

"We had soup. There was salad and cake but we didn't want any. I'll tell Beulah to put the things away."

"We saw the specialist," Irene told her. "I didn't like him. He said Judy Irene's skin isn't delicate and he says my doctor should never have prescribed powdered milk for her. He says she should have Grade A milk with malt-something or other. I don't remember but Dale has it down. It's a lot more work than the powdered milk formula. I'm going to *need* a nursemaid if everything he says is true. Did anyone call in answer to that ad?"

"Yes, but no one I thought would do."

"Tell them to come out to the house anyway," Irene said. "There might be some *I* like. Tell them to come after five though," she added. "We won't be home 'til then. The baby got all tired out after the specialist fin-

ished examining her and he said she could finish her nap here in his waiting room. I'm tired
too."

"Don't feel you have to hurry home. I'll
take care of everything," Judy said almost too
willingly. " 'Bye, Irene."

She had hardly closed the conversation when
the telephone rang again.

"Someone else answering the ad," Judy explained to Peter after she had hung up. "I
told her to come out at five. Irene wants to interview the nursemaids herself. Maybe I can
persuade her not to take them because they
have babies."

"But suppose she sees the ad?"

"She mustn't, Peter. We'll simply have to
pray that she doesn't look."

"And that the telephone keeps on ringing.
There it goes again!"

"Take it, Peter. Let's take turns answering
it. We'll make a game of it and the one who
hears Jane's voice wins."

"And if we don't hear it, we both lose," Peter said as he picked up the telephone and began speaking into it. He closed the conversation with, "I don't suppose you'll do, but you
may as well come out. Mrs. Meredith will see
you at five o'clock."

Judy's turn came next; then Peter's. Each
time they turned away from the telephone dis-

appointed. By the end of the afternoon they had a list of applicants consisting of a colored woman with a four year old boy, a childless woman who insisted she was a good nurse, a German woman with twins, three other women with babies ranging in age from three months to seven years and two women who refused to give either their names or the ages of their children. Their voices sounded very unlike Jane's but Judy grasped at the straw and gave out the address anyway.

"Jane might be one of them, though I doubt it. How many are coming altogether?" she asked Peter.

He counted them up.

"I believe it's a dozen at least. You'll have a busy afternoon."

"Will I!" exclaimed Judy. "I'll be busy all right, trying to persuade Irene not to engage any of them." And suddenly Judy began to laugh almost hysterically. "Peter, isn't it funny? I just realized that *this* is my vacation."

She was still laughing about it when Dale and Irene came in. Dale was holding the baby and Irene was holding—Judy's heart stood still. The paper! She had seen the ad.

CHAPTER XXIII

THE DEATH OF AN AD

"You think this is funny, don't you?" Irene cried, thrusting the paper almost in Judy's face. "You think you've played a good joke on me advertising for a nursemaid with a baby. But I know why you did it. You're trying to find Jane! Even though I asked you not to, you went ahead and put this ad in the paper anyway. Well, I'll tell you one thing, Judy Bolton, if she does answer it her husband isn't going to know about it. Depend on that!"

"Of course. I—I didn't think he would."

"Don't you suppose he can read papers too? If he sees that ad he'll know we're trying to find Jane and he'll come here and start making trouble. The ad's so big he could hardly miss it. Besides," Irene added, "I have to have a nursemaid. I don't suppose a single person is coming out today."

"You're wrong there, Irene," Judy told her. "I did ask some of them to come out."

"How many?" Irene wanted to know.

"About twelve."

"Twelve!" she exclaimed in great dismay.

"Twelve women with yelling babies, as Dale calls them. If this house isn't bedlam already it soon will be. But this is the last time! No more advertising for women with babies after today. I'm going to write a new ad and telephone it in myself."

And with that she sat down at the desk without taking time to remove her hat or coat and began writing furiously. In the meantime Dale, looking like the ghost of his former self, had taken the baby upstairs. They heard him telling Beulah to attend to her. Beulah, who admitted she knew nothing whatsoever about babies!

"There it is!" Irene announced when she had finished writing the ad. She handed it to Judy and she and Peter read it together:

NURSEMAID, competent, experienced with young baby. Good position in private home. PARKVILLE 6–7675.

"Now, Peter," Irene directed, "since you put the other ad in, you'd better tell me how many papers are running it so that I can see that it is canceled. Oh, dear!" she broke off. "There's one of the nursemaids now." She had seen a woman with a baby in her arms turning in at the walk. "Perhaps you'd better do the telephoning after all, Peter. But no tricks," Irene warned him. "This time the ad goes in just the way I've written it."

"I'll take care of it," Peter answered gravely.

He was busy calling up the papers when Judy let the first applicant in. Others followed in rapid succession and Irene had a time quieting them after informing them that it was a mistake and she hadn't wanted a nursemaid with a baby after all.

Neither of the two who had refused to give their names turned out to be Jane. They were both foreigners whose names would have been difficult to make out over the telephone.

At last Irene had disposed of them all except one gaunt, old-maidish individual. She was the one who had been so insistent. She had no child of her own and looked as though she had no understanding of children. But Irene told her she might do.

"Call again tomorrow at this same time," she said, "and I'll take you unless some more experienced woman applies for the position. You say you've never cared for a baby as young as mine."

"Two years is the youngest I've cared for, but I have references."

"I'll look at them tomorrow."

And when she was gone Irene turned to Judy with a sigh.

"All right, you fix Judy Irene's new formula. You thought the specialist was such a good idea. Maybe you will understand it. I'm going to lie down."

The new formula was hard to fix. Judy had to admit that. The malt mixture was supposed to dissolve in the warm milk but it took stirring and pressing and chopping with a spoon to dissolve it. The baby liked the new milk, however, and as Judy held the bottle for her, she gurgled and seemed quite contented. Peter looked in at the door and his eyes twinkled mischievously.

"Not bad," he commented. "Why don't you apply for the position yourself?"

Judy glared at him. "Before I'd accept a position in this house I'd—I'd——"

"I wouldn't advise the East River," he chuckled. "It's too dirty. Gas smells bad and as for poison——"

"Peter!" Judy's eyes became wide and terrified. "Do you suppose Jane could have— Jane and the baby——"

"Oh, darling, I'm sorry! I only meant it as a joke. But how stupid of me!"

"Not at all." But Judy's voice was stricken. And there were no more jokes between them that day. With the ad gone out of the papers their last hope of finding Jane had vanished. Dale was closeted in his room. It would have

been impossible to talk with him, anyway,
Judy knew. She supposed Irene might as well
hire a nursemaid and she and Peter might as
well go home. But at the thought of going
home despair settled over Judy like a fog. She
couldn't. She had been the cause of the whole
tragic mix-up. She must stay until at least a
semblance of happiness had been restored to
Tower House.

The following day the telephone rang almost
constantly and Irene answered every call.
Judy helped by taking care of the baby and
forced herself to be cheerful. Peter just hung
around, going out occasionally for a breath of
air and taking Judy with him whenever she
could be spared. They talked of things that
didn't matter, commenting on queer cupolas
and fancy fretwork on many of the older
houses in Parkville. Occasionally a FOR
SALE sign or a new apartment building told
them that this section would soon be built up
like the rest of Brooklyn. It seemed sad, somehow. Everything they talked about seemed sad
as it was all colored by what they were thinking. Jane would never be found. Dale would
work himself into a nervous breakdown carrying the weight of this secret. Suddenly Judy
said,

"Peter, I know you don't like promises, but
I want you to swear to this. When we're mar-

ried, no matter what goes wrong, I want to know it. If it's your business or—or whatever it is. Even if anything as dreadful as this should happen to us, I want to know. You'll promise that, won't you? It's the only way we can ever be happy."

"Yes, Judy, I promise."

They returned to the house sober and thoughtful. Already the living room was beginning to fill with nursemaids to be interviewed. Judy left it to Irene.

"You might do," she heard her saying. "Two hundred a month! Heavens, do nursemaids charge that much? I thought, with a room to yourself and everything . . . No, I'm afraid not."

Two or three applicants came with babies. These were promptly told the position was not available. Judy supposed they had seen the ad that was put in the papers on the previous day. Could there still be some hope of Jane's seeing it? But, as the day dragged on, even that ray of hope faded.

Toward the end of the day Irene came up to the nursery where Judy was struggling with the baby's feedings again.

"I'm ready to collapse," she said. "I managed to get rid of that awful old maid from yesterday and the insolent young woman with the peacock feather in her hat. But there are three women still waiting in the living room. I've got to decide on one of them but I can't make up my mind. You do it, Judy. You're still a good judge of people."

"Thanks, Irene. I'll do my best," Judy promised and went downstairs.

Three rather impatient women looked up as she entered the living room. One of them was young and attractive but had a superior way about her that Judy definitely disliked. The second was a comfortable looking woman well past middle age. She protested when Judy told her the nursery was on the third floor.

"Couldn't it be moved?" she asked. "My heart won't stand running up and down stairs all day."

"I'm afraid not," Judy said and turned to the third applicant. Just then the door bell rang. She called to Peter.

"See who it is and if it's someone applying for this position, show her in."

Peter nodded and went out. He did not return for several moments and Judy, supposing the bell had been rung by a peddler, continued interviewing the last of the three remaining applicants.

"Experienced?"

"Yes, m'am. I worked for a woman in Manhattan for five years and then her child started in school and she didn't need me. Here's her reference. And then I took care of twins until they grew up. They were perfect darlings," she added. "Their mother was glad to give me a reference."

Judy read the references, then looked up again. The woman seemed efficient, reliable. Her manner was pleasing though rather abrupt. She was about to say, "You'll do," when Peter, his face beaming, stepped into the room from a rear door.

"Sorry, ladies," he announced, his voice elaborately casual. "The position is filled."

Immediately all three women began firing questions at Judy.

"What is this? A joke on us? Or do you think we have nothing better to do with our time than to run around looking for positions that are already taken? What about our carfare out here? What about the day lost when we could have found a good place——"

"Here's your carfare. Now please go," Judy entreated at last. She handed them each a dime and they seemed to take even that as an insult.

"What about the time we spent here?"

"That's to be expected. I have your address," she said to the woman she had been about to engage. "I'll call you if——"

"I'm afraid I shan't be available," the

woman snapped and followed the others out of the door.

Judy turned to Peter, hardly daring to hope she had read his look correctly.

"Well, Angel," he said. "I win the game. She's here. One of the papers obliged us by inserting a comma. You see the difference it makes."

And Peter handed Judy a clipping. The ad which should have read:

NURSEMAID, competent, experienced, with young baby . . . had been changed to read:

NURSEMAID, competent, experienced, with young baby . . .

And there by the dining room window standing right where a beam of light fell across her face, was Jane with a young baby in her arms.

CHAPTER XXIV

THE NEW NURSEMAID

"Jane!" cried Judy. "Jane, *dear!* You can't imagine how glad I am to see you. Here, let me take the baby while we talk."

And, saying this, Judy took her own little namesake, Judy Irene, into her arms. She kissed the top of the little golden head and all at once tears began streaming down her face.

"Take her, Peter. I'm going to cry all over her," she managed to say.

Jane stood there looking bewildered.

"I don't understand," she said at last. "I didn't speak to you over the telephone. I spoke to some woman who advertised for a nursemaid. I didn't tell her about the baby."

"That was Irene," Judy said. "And it's a good thing you didn't tell her about the baby. Oh, I forgot to introduce you, but this young man who so thoughtfully escorted you in at the side entrance is Peter Dobbs. We are—we were engaged."

"We still are," he corrected her, giving her a look that was meant to banish, for all time, any doubt she had about their engagement.

The lost diamond seemed a trifling matter, even to Judy, now that they had found Jane and Judy Irene. But a difficult task still lay ahead of them—telling her and then breaking the news to Irene.

"Irene didn't recognize my voice, and no wonder," said Jane. "I have such a cold. I'm not fit to apply for a position looking after anybody's baby. I'm not fit to look after my own, even. But I thought if I could just rest a little, I'd be better soon and then—oh, I know I could look after Irene's baby the way she wants it looked after. We could bring up Judy Irene and little Jane to be twin friends just the way we always said we would. Really, it's like an answer to a prayer."

"It is an answer to a prayer," said Judy in all sincerity.

Jane looked at her tear-stained face. A little frown of puzzlement appeared between her brows as she said, "But what I don't understand is why you should be so glad to see me. Why, you hardly knew me! It was Irene and I who were such friends."

"You will understand it," Judy promised. "But first let's make the baby comfortable. She can lie in the carriage in the living room while we talk in here. Just a minute and I'll fix her."

Peter was still holding the baby. As Judy

took her from him she looked carefully to see if she still wore her hospital bracelet. But no. Someone must have removed it.

"I see the baby isn't wearing her hospital bracelet," Judy commented after she had returned to the dining room where Peter and Jane sat by the table talking.

"You mean those beads?" Jane asked. "I thought they were too tight and cut the string. They fell apart but I intend to restring them as a keepsake. The bracelets were pretty, weren't they?"

"Yes," Judy said quietly, "they were."

"And useful too," Peter added. "You realize, of course, that without those bracelets there would be no way of telling whether or not you had your own baby or—or some other child."

Jane laughed.

"Indeed there would! Do you think for a single minute I wouldn't know my own precious little Jane? Why, there isn't another baby in the world as lovely as she is with her golden hair and big blue eyes."

"What about Irene's baby?" Peter asked.

"Of course, she was lovely too. The nurses told us that our babies were the prettiest——"

She paused. A footfall sounded on the stairs almost above their heads. Judy whispered, "It's Irene," and put her finger to her lips.

In a moment they heard Irene coming into

the living room. They kept perfectly quiet and listened.

"Lambikins!" they heard her crooning over the carriage. "Mother's precious! You look better already. Did the new nursemaid take good care of Mother's little Judy?"

"She thinks it's her baby," Jane whispered. "Sh!"

Again Judy put her finger to her lips. But at that moment a wailing cry sounded from the nursery upstairs. Almost tipping her chair over in her hurry to reach Irene, Judy fairly flew into the living room. Irene was as pale as a ghost.

"The house is haunted," she declared in a hollow voice. "I heard Judy Irene crying upstairs and she can't be upstairs because she's here!"

"Are you—are you sure?" asked Judy, at a loss for words herself.

"Sure she's here? What are you saying, Judy? Can't you see Judy Irene lying right here in the carriage? But how much better she looks. Her hair is brushed so neatly and it looks all shiny, the way it used to look in the hospital. The new nursemaid must be a good one."

"She is," Judy said. "Irene, the new nursemaid is Jane. That was Jane's baby you heard crying upstairs."

In the dining room Jane started to protest but Peter whispered, "Judy's having a little fun. She's trying to find out if Irene knows her own baby."

"I don't think it's fun. I'm going to tell her."

"Not now," Peter urged. "There is something we must do before you say anything. Have you those beads from your baby's bracelet? Let's string them quickly and put them back on her arm."

"That is a good idea," Jane agreed. "I suppose I shouldn't have taken them off in the first place. Suppose the babies did get mixed——"

"There isn't time for supposing now," Peter told her, still in a whisper. "Let's hurry. Judy!" he called more loudly. "Come here and help me find a needle and a stout piece of thread!"

"Gladly. Excuse me, Irene. Peter's probably lost a button. And please don't be angry with me. Jane *will* make a good nursemaid and her husband's people won't find her here and even if they do Peter says they can't make trouble when she's supporting herself and the baby. Don't disappoint her. She needs work so badly. What would she do without it?"

"What has she done since she left the hospital? She's managed all right, hasn't she?"

"Judy, hurry!" Peter called insistently.

Judy broke away. She knew where Irene kept her sewing things but, when she saw what they were doing, Jane had to thread the needle. Judy's hand trembled so.

Jane slipped a few plain pink beads on the needle and said, "I'll begin the name now. Do you see an *M*?"

Judy handed her a bead with the letter *M* on it. Next came an *E;* then an *R* and then another *E*.

"But that's wrong," Jane protested. "It should be another *R* for *Merrit*. But where did the *E* come from? There's only one *E* in my name."

"Go on stringing the beads just as Judy hands them to you," Peter directed quietly.

Jane slipped the *E* on her needle, looking dazed. Then the *D, I, T,* and *H* in rapid succession. She stared at them a moment and then fell forward, striking her head on the table before Peter could catch her.

"Get a doctor," he spoke hoarsely to Judy. "Get Irene's doctor, the one she had when she was in the hospital."

"What's the matter?" asked Irene from the doorway.

"Jane's fainted. That's all." He lifted her in his arms and carried her in to the sofa. "She'll come to in a minute. But she ought to have a doctor. I'll call your doctor if you'll give me his name and telephone number."

"It's Dr. Bishop. I'll dial it," Irene offered.
"I know the number by heart."

She dialed and then let Peter talk while she
hurried back to Jane. Judy was mopping her
face with cold water and Dale, who had heard
the disturbance, stood by the sofa like a man in
a trance.

"She was hungry. That's what it was,"
Irene spoke rapidly. "Poor girl, she was
nearly starved. And here I was blaming you
for trying to find her. You were right, Judy.
You're always right and I hope you can forgive me."

Judy squeezed her hand affectionately,
afraid to think of what would happen next.

"There's nothing to forgive, dear," she said.
"It was all a misunderstanding. And still is,"
she added under her breath.

Jane was beginning to stir a little. Now she
opened her eyes.

"Too many people around here," Dale said
hurriedly as he pulled Irene away. Judy could
see that he still had the confused notion that
she couldn't be told. But how could they keep
from telling her?

"Let's go up to the nursery and see Jane's
baby," Irene now suggested. "Come on, Judy.
Peter will stay with Jane until the doctor
comes."

CHAPTER XXV

IN THE TOWER NURSERY

AT THE nursery door Judy stood perfectly still as Dale and Irene went in together. Irene took one long look at the baby she had believed to be her own.

"How alike they are," she said. "I never realized the two babies looked so much alike. But I'd know Judy Irene. Her hair is more golden."

"Yes," Judy said, daring to breathe again. "It is, isn't it?"

"Let's take the babies downstairs and compare them," Dale suggested. "You know, they took their footprints at the hospital so there isn't any doubt——"

"Who said there was?" Irene interrupted sharply. "And who wants to be taking two tiny babies back and forth to the hospital to compare their footprints? They'll simply have to wear their hospital bracelets all the time to keep them from getting mixed. Come to think of it, Judy Irene hasn't been wearing her bracelet. Do either of you know what happened to it?"

"I do," Judy spoke up quickly. "Dale cut it off her arm and I put it away. The beads will need restringing but it won't take a minute to do it."

"You do it," Dale said, a relieved look coming over his face. "And then bring the baby down. Irene is coming into my study a minute. I want her to see the story I'm writing."

"Oh, Dale! Not now," she protested. "Not with Jane sick downstairs and the doctor coming any minute——"

"Yes, *now,*" he interrupted in the same commanding tone he had used to Judy. And Irene followed him.

Left alone, Judy dug frantic fingers into the loose dirt around the primrose plant. Luckily she didn't need to restring the bracelet—only to wash it. This she did quickly and left it on the radiator to dry while she tiptoed softly downstairs and picked up the bracelet Jane had dropped when she fainted. Like a flash it came to her what she must do. She glanced at Judy Irene sleeping in the carriage. But Peter stopped her before she had taken a single step in that direction.

"Could she tell?" he whispered so that the still half-conscious Jane on the sofa could not hear him.

Judy shook her head.

"Okay," he said. "Everything may yet

work out. Now I understand about the bracelet. Judy, you've been a trump.''

"So've you," she told him hastily, darting toward the carriage where, praying that it would work, she fastened the right bracelet on Judy Irene's arm. When it was fastened the baby stirred a little in her sleep and the beads clinked against each other. Judy thought she had never heard a sweeter sound.

Upstairs the bracelet on the radiator dried quickly. Judy had just finished fastening it to little Jane's arm when she heard the doctor's car stopping before the door. She picked up little Jane and hurried back downstairs.

It took the doctor only a moment to diagnose Jane's case as simple shock. He understood the reason when Judy told him, as briefly as she could, how the babies had been accidentally exchanged. By the time she had finished explaining it, Jane was sitting up and listening.

"And it was my fault," she said in self-accusation. "I'm the one who picked up the wrong baby. But I wouldn't have done it if HE hadn't hurried me so.''

"Then I should say it was HIS fault, whoever HE is," the doctor said in a kind voice.

"HE is my husband. *Was* my husband," Jane amended. "I'm never going back to him and I can't stand his mother——''

"And you, my dear little lady, must put all

such thoughts out of your head," the doctor interrupted gently. "You have a home here and now you have your own baby——"

"My own baby?" Jane questioned dazedly.

"Of course," Judy said and put little Jane into her arms.

Jane looked at her for a moment, stroked her light brown hair; then sighed, "She's beautiful, isn't she?" and lay back on the sofa with the baby still in her arms.

The doctor smiled.

"She'll be all right," he said. "But what about Mrs. Meredith? Does she know?"

"Not yet," Judy answered.

"Well, is it necessary to tell her?"

Judy and Peter looked at each other.

"Well, is it?" Peter asked.

Judy shook her head slowly. "I don't see why. I've put their bracelets on correctly. You see," she explained to the doctor, "we hid the bracelet when we found we had the wrong baby. Mrs. Meredith's husband was afraid to tell her."

"That is fortunate," the doctor said. "Mrs. Merrit is used to shocks, I gather. Life hasn't been altogether smooth for her. But she has a strong constitution. She has learned how to take it. Now it's quite a different story when it comes to telling Mrs. Meredith. Her father's death was a severe shock and I saw how she reacted to that. She has a delicate constitution and, I might say, a hereditary tendency to magnify her troubles. No, I should think it would be very unwise to subject her to any unnecessary shock. Her heart might not stand it."

"Then Dale was right," Judy said, "and I was so angry with him."

"You mean," Jane asked from the sofa, "that you don't intend to tell Irene anything— anything at all?"

"Well, that depends. I know these two can keep the secret." The doctor indicated Judy and Peter. "They've done pretty well so far. But you, Mrs. Merril, haven't you grown rather attached to Mrs. Meredith's baby?"

"Of course. I love it like my very own, but then," Jane added, "I should. I'm going to be its nursemaid."

"And I prophesy you'll be a good one."

"I hope to do my best, doctor. We'll bring our babies up like twins."

"Dr. Bishop," Irene hailed him from the stairs. "I heard that. Isn't she a dream of a nursemaid? Our babies will be twin friends just the way we always said they would be. And she'll live here with me and we'll have such good times. We'll wheel our babies together and maybe, sometimes, Dale won't mind looking after both of them while we go to the movies——"

Dale was just behind her.

"Mind!" he interrupted. "Why, I'll be proud to look after them."

"But no stories on such evenings," Irene warned him. "I know you when you're deep in a story. And Dale," she pleaded, "don't ever write another story like the one you just showed me. It has the most vicious character in it. Dale called it 'The Beast of Boston' and actually, it made him a little like a beast himself to write such a story. I helped him tear it up."

"Good work," said Peter.

"Excellent work, I should say," Judy agreed.

"And would you believe it, Dr. Bishop," Irene went on, "while he was under the influence of this beast he actually persuaded me to take the baby to another doctor and now she has the messiest formula. It takes ages to fix it and the food won't dissolve and it sticks all over the pans——"

"We'll soon fix that," Dr. Bishop interrupted with a twinkle in his eye and he began writing out a formula.

"Why, it's just like the one she had before. It gave her the colic dreadfully——"

"It won't this time," the doctor interrupted.

Irene turned to Dale.

"Do you mind?"

"Not at all," he answered heartily. "Dr. Bishop knows what he's doing. Better let him take a look at your baby while he's here, Jane."

"My baby's all right," she said cuddling it.

"But you? Are you all right now?" Irene asked anxiously. "Doctor, what made her faint?"

"It often happens," he answered brusquely. "I must be going now. Call me up if you need me." And, bidding them goodbye, he hurried away.

"Well, I know what it was," Irene said, turning to Jane. "He didn't need to tell me. You haven't been getting enough to eat, but dinner's ready now and, if you feel strong enough to come to the table——"

"I feel as strong as an ox," laughed Jane. "Here, take your baby——" She giggled. "I mean *my* baby. I want to see them together just once before we go in. You know, we always told them apart because Jane's hair was darker—There, it is!" she finished, seeing them together. "But aren't they both beautiful?"

Peter and Judy glanced at each other. Everything had worked out so much better than they had thought possible. It sobered them to think of what might have happened. But Peter never stayed serious for long. After dinner, when they were alone, he suddenly burst out laughing.

"Well, Judy," he asked. "When are you going to hang out your shingle?"

"My—what? What on earth are you talking about?"

"I just remembered the carrot and how you said something was going to be mixed. Well, it was, wasn't it? And you promised to hang out a shingle and pose as Judy, the Mystic, if you were right."

"Silly," she scolded fondly. "If I could tell things that easily I'd say a charm and find my diamond. We can't keep secrets from your grandmother, you know, and she's going to feel terribly when she hears that I've lost it."

CHAPTER XXVI

GOODBYE TO TOWER HOUSE

A WEEK later Judy, preparing to leave in Peter's car, paused in her packing. Jane stood at the door, a baby on either shoulder.

"Judy," she said, "I came to thank you. I'm not sure I thanked you properly before. I don't know whether or not I can. But nothing could be more wonderful than living right here for the rest of my life—with both my babies. I'll always think of them both as mine and Irene says she'll always think of them both as hers. She says Jane has a look in her eyes so like Judy—" She giggled. "But isn't it funny? She still doesn't know."

"There's no reason why she ever should," Judy said, repeating the exact words Dale had spoken to her. "But there's one thing that I've been wondering, Jane. Would you mind telling me?"

"I'll tell you anything," Jane declared warmly. "I have no secrets but this one."

"Then tell me where you were all the time we were looking for you. I know you didn't go back to the apartment——"

"I couldn't," Jane said. "I knew they'd have it watched."

"They did all right." And Judy told her about their adventure with Lady Isabel and the detective. They had gone into the nursery together and the two babies went to sleep while she told it. She even told Jane she had what Ludwig Bull had called "Evidence in the Merrit Case" and how his son had broken into the apartment and also into her father's office.

"But what did he do that for?" asked Jane.

"I think," Judy said, "that he needed a doctor to testify in court before they could prove that you—well, that you weren't able to care for your own baby. Of course, no real doctor would testify to such a thing. So they stole a card my father had——"

"Your father? Was he the doctor I went to when I used to have those nervous crying spells? He's the one who suggested I come to New York and found me the loveliest place to live. That was all I needed, he said, a change of scene."

"Yes," Judy said. "That was my father. Well, Jane, I think this lawyer had an idea that one of his friends could pretend to be my father and offer those cards as evidence. My father had diagnosed your case as *neurasthenia* and a crook lawyer could easily misconstrue that and make a judge believe it meant that you were mentally unbalanced. But don't worry,'' Judy went on hurriedly. ''With Dr. Bishop and my father on your side, Ludwig Bull has decided to drop the case. Peter found out that much yesterday.''

''Good! Then even if my husband does find me he can't make me go back to his mother's.''

''No, and Peter found out something else too. They've left for a trip—the whole Merrit family. I guess they thought it was a good time to take a trip. So if you still have any use for the things in the apartment you can send for them with perfect safety. But, Jane,'' she went on, ''you still didn't answer my question. I know you weren't at the apartment. But where were you?''

''That's easy,'' Jane answered. ''I rented a room——''

''But how could you?'' Judy asked. ''Did the landlady trust you?''

''She didn't need to,'' Jane said. ''I paid a week's rent and I had my meals sent up from a restaurant. The money wouldn't have lasted very long though. I can assure you I needed this position.''

''But, Jane,'' Judy protested. ''I thought your husband took possession of your pocket-book.''

"I bought another. It was the pocketbook I carried those beads in. You remember?"

"But how could you buy a pocketbook? How could you buy *anything* without money?"

"That," said Jane, "is the part you won't believe. But since I promised, I'll tell you anyway. I pawned a diamond."

"Oh, I see. You had a diamond ring——"

"No. No," Jane objected. "I hadn't any jewelry of any kind. I didn't say it was a ring I pawned, just a diamond. Believe it or not, I found it inside the baby's bunting. But don't ask me how it got there. I don't know."

"Jane! Did you save the pawn ticket?"

"I think so. I borrowed a hundred dollars on it. There's still over fifty left. But what makes you look at me so, Judy? You can't think it was wrong to pawn a diamond I found when—when I'd have starved if I hadn't. And anybody that would own a diamond that size certainly didn't need it as much as I needed something to eat and a place for the baby and me to sleep and—and money for carfare and newspapers so I could look for a job."

"But suppose—" Judy hesitated. "Suppose the diamond fell out of someone's engagement ring?"

"Why, then it ought to be returned, of course. I guess it ought to be returned anyway," Jane decided, "now that I have a posi-

tion. You couldn't call this lovely place a job,
could you, Judy? I could easily save enough to
redeem that diamond out of my wages. But
how could I find the owner?"

"Wait a minute and I'll show you!"

Like a flash, Judy was out of the nursery,
into her own room and back again with her
ring. She had taken it off her finger at Peter's
request. He had asked her not to wear it until
he could save enough to replace the diamond.
But now he wouldn't need to.

"You see," Judy said, showing Jane the
empty setting. "It was somebody's engagement ring. I thought I lost it on the stairs at
the hospital but I must have lost it in the room
when I was putting on Judy Irene's bunting.
I was so excited and happy that my hand was
trembling. I remember that."

"Oh, my dear!" Jane exclaimed. "I'm so
sorry I pawned it."

"Well, I'm not," Judy answered. "I loved
the ring in the first place because it had belonged to Peter's grandmother and there was a
story connected with it. Now there's another.
Believe me, Jane, it will mean so much more to
me because it helped you when you were in
trouble."

"I think you mean that," Jane said slowly.
"And I think I know now why Peter calls you
'Angel.' But here, take the money I have

and—oh, good! Here's the ticket. I'll make up the rest of it to you as soon as I can."

"There's no hurry. Just consider it as a loan and keep out a good-sized reward——"

"Reward? Now Judy," Jane scolded. "That is carrying it a little too far. I am the one who should be rewarding you."

Judy took the pawn ticket and the money Jane had given her. By adding to it what there was left in her purse and the check her father had given her, there was just enough—with nine cents left over. The man in the pawnshop replaced the prongs on the ring and reset the diamond. He said it had simply fallen out of the setting because the prongs that held it were worn out. It often happened with an old ring.

It was not until the following day when she and Peter were ready to start for home that she told him. He carried her suitcases out to the car but she returned to the porch where she said goodbye to Jane and Irene a second time. She kissed both girls affectionately and gave Dale a long handclasp. He knew what it meant. She would never tell his secret.

Next, she ran inside and kissed both babies, alike as two roses as they slept in their new twin carriage. Her kisses were as light as the baby dreams that must have drifted around their heads—dreams of growing up together—

of being twin friends. Would Judy Irene, Judy wondered, ever guess why her nursemaid loved her as dearly as her own mother did. No, she probably never would. She'd just take it for granted. A child as sweet as Judy Irene would expect to be loved. So would little Jane. Dale, wonderfully kind and tender to her now, would take the place of a father. And happiness would reign once more in Tower House.

"Ready, Angel?" Peter called from the car.

"I'm ready," Judy called back to him joyously. "Really ready," she added when they were in the car. "I haven't forgotten a thing —not even my diamond."

She held up her hand, her eyes shining as brightly as the gleaming stone on her finger.

"Judy! You've found it?"

"Yes," she answered softly, "and Peter, I've changed my mind about secrets. Sometimes they're quite—quite beautiful. Look back at Tower House if you don't believe it. Look at those happy faces. But suppose we had told Irene and her heart was too weak to stand the shock——"

"Don't suppose," Peter said. "Just be thankful that everything happened as it did. We're on our way home now and we're leaving no heartaches behind us. Let's hope there'll be none ahead."

"We have to have some," Judy said logically. "You and I couldn't be married and live together all our lives without having a single one. It might even be a little dull, like having no more mysteries to solve. Peter," she added wistfully, "I wonder where we will live. Everybody's been asking me. Have you any idea?"

"Only a vague one," Peter confessed. But, could Judy have read his thoughts, she would have known that his vague idea was more of a reality than she supposed. The house with its strange new mystery, THE CLUE IN THE PATCHWORK QUILT, was waiting. But like Judy herself, the future kept its secret.